# JILTED BY JACK FROST

A Yule Be Mine Monster Romance

Alexa Ashe

Jilted by Jack Frost

Copyright © 2024 by Alexa Ashe

All rights reserved.

No portion of this book may be reproduced, distributed, or transmitted in any form or by any means, including photocopying, recording, or other electronic or mechanical means, without the prior written permission from the publisher or author, except for the use of brief quotations in book reviews.

This book is a work of fiction. The characters and events in this book are fictitious. Any similarity to persons, living or dead, real or fictional, is purely coincidental and not intended by the author.

https://www.facebook.com/authoralexaashe

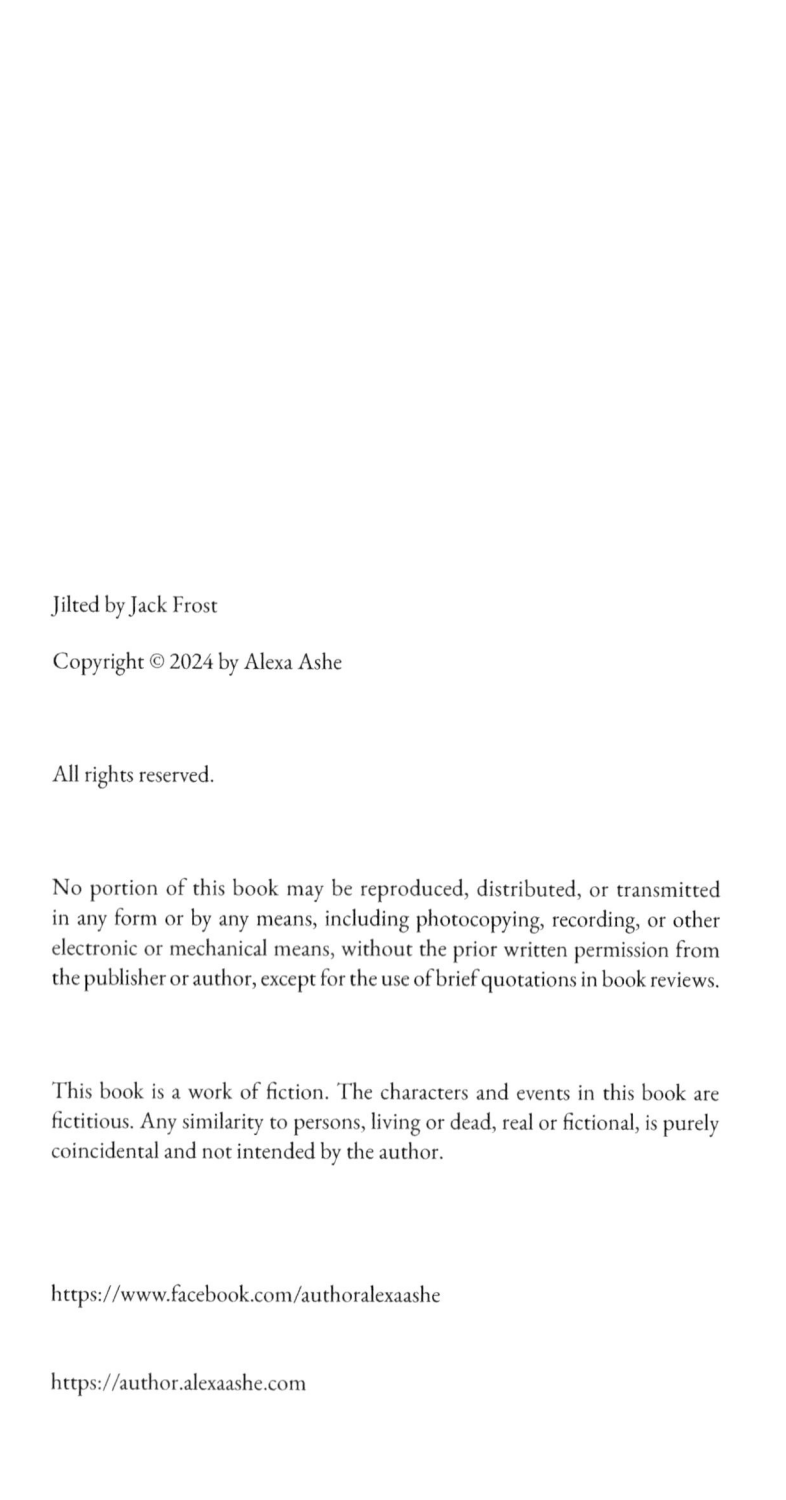

https://author.alexaashe.com

# CONTENTS

1. Violet — 1
2. Violet — 8
3. Jack — 16
4. Violet — 23
5. Violet — 31
6. Jack — 38
7. Violet — 45
8. Jack — 49
9. Violet — 56
10. Jack — 62
11. Violet — 70
12. Violet — 80
13. Jack — 87
14. Violet — 94

| | | |
|---|---|---|
| 15. | Violet | 102 |
| 16. | Jack | 111 |
| 17. | Violet | 117 |
| 18. | Jack | 127 |
| 19. | Violet | 135 |
| 20. | Violet | 141 |
| 21. | Jack | 152 |
| 22. | Violet | 159 |
| 23. | Jack | 176 |
| 24. | Violet | 181 |
| 25. | Jack | 192 |
| What's Next | | 196 |
| About Author | | 205 |

## Chapter One

# Violet

As the snow collects on the ground outside, the only thing I'm thinking about is that I would rather perform my own brain surgery than stay even a minute past my shift.

Seeing as I'm a nurse and *not* a neurosurgeon, my chances at survival are far slimmer than one might think.

I miss my memory foam mattress. And when I finally clock out in five hours, I'm not going to spend the night on a hospital bed. I don't care if I have to walk home through six feet of snow to get there. I'm leaving, but I need snow pants, stat.

Alana shoves a white cheddar flavored chip in her mouth and sighs. "Looks like the snow is sticking."

"As it always does in Salida," I mutter. This time of year, any Colorado snow was bound to stick. Normally, I love snow. I love how it's beautiful, cold, pure, and I love how it gives me an excuse to not get to work if I'm stuck at home.

What I don't love, however, is that it looks like I will now be stuck at work instead.

"It's supposed to be a blizzard," Alana adds. "Worst we've seen in years, according to Chief."

"Is he a meteorologist now?" I ask, turning to look at her with an amused smile on my face.

She laughs and shakes her head. "No. But his sister is."

Oh. Great.

"How much begging do you think I'd have to do to go home early?" I ask Alana, stealing a chip out of her bag and tossing it into my mouth.

"Let's see," Alana says, tapping her chin. Then she counts off each point she makes on her fingers. "We're already severely understaffed on a good day. Lilah is out on maternity leave. There's a literal blizzard forecasted, which means there's going to be an influx of car accidents and likely some dumbass farmers with frostbite."

My expression morphs into one of devastation. "So... unlikely, then?"

"You're more likely to get cuffed to the reception desk than you are to be allowed to go home, Vi."

I grimace.

"Oh, come on. This is what we signed up for, right? We wanted to help people. That's exactly what we'll be doing tonight."

She's right. I came into this job because I wanted to help people. I loved the idea of clocking into the work and spending twelve hours doing nothing but offering everything I have to anyone who needs it.

But I also can't ignore the way I feel—like this job might not be enough for me anymore. And God, do I feel guilty about that. Really, I do. I hate that giving my all to anyone who steps inside this hospital isn't... fulfilling anymore. This used to be everything I ever wanted. Even in middle school, Alana and I knew that this was what we wanted.

So why do I feel like I need more than this? Being a nurse was everything I've ever wanted, even a year ago. But that's changed. Or maybe I'm what's changed.

It's not that I'm not happy, because I am. I get to go to work and be the person who puts a smile on the faces of those who desperately need it, and I get to do it with my best friend.

But I know, deep in my heart, that there's more out there. I know that there's more to this world than this town where I've spent most of my life. I know I want to be a part of something more.

I just don't know if I ever will.

Pasting on a smile, I nod. "Yeah, you're right. But I sure will miss my flannel sheets."

Alana grins. "Just five more hours."

"Fine," I say. "But you've got to go change Mrs. Bradford's bedpan after lunch."

She makes a face and huffs out a breath.

"You always make me do bedpans when we're on shift together."

I smile cheekily and bat my lashes. "That's because I have seniority."

"You were here *one* month before me, Violet Jones."

"Bedpans are the price you pay for your vacation in Hawaii with your boyfriend, unfortunately."

Alana hesitates, then shrugs.

"Worth it."

I go back to staring out the window, not bothering to hide my disgust. "Blizzard or no, I'm walking out of this hospital immediately after clocking out."

"Violet, no."

"Alana, yes," I reply, nodding aggressively. "I live two blocks from here. Hell, I walked to work this morning. Literally nothing will keep me here past midnight, Alana."

"They're going to find your ice-covered body in a ditch three miles from here tomorrow morning."

I debate it for a moment. "That's still preferable to spending the night here."

She shakes her head and clicks her tongue. "You're insane."

"I'm determined," I correct.

"Insanely determined," she amends.

Laughing, I turn away from the window and face her. Alana's messy bun is more messy than bun at this point, but somehow she makes it look good. I blame it on her gorgeous blonde curls and the facial features her equally gorgeous mother passed down to her.

I, on the other hand, am the brown-haired, round-cheeked version of my father. Same mossy green eyes, though mine are doe-eyed like my mothers, same straight nose, same smile, with my top lip just slightly smaller than the bottom. We even share the same freckle that sits just below our jaws on our necks.

We're both quiet for a long moment, but then I say, "When am I going to get to go to Hawaii?"

Alana snorts and hands me her bag of chips. "It's not my fault you're not living your best life, babe. You could always join me on a vacation to Cancun! I could use someone to help me keep the boys in check."

"Ah, yes. Because I'm renowned for my charming personality and social finesse," I reply, pretending to contemplate. "That might be a dangerous mix."

We both laugh, and I add, "But maybe I *should* start planning a getaway."

She turns her head to look over her shoulder before saying, "I've got to get back to work. How much longer is your break?"

I pull my phone out of my pocket and check the time. "A solid six minutes."

"Perfect. Gives me just enough time to change Mrs. Bradford's bedpan before you and I sneak into the operating theater and catch the tail end of the laparotomy Brad's doing?"

Brad, her current boyfriend, is a surgeon. They're the cutest, most vomit-inducing couple I've ever met, and I've been their third wheel for a little while now.

Because it's always just been me. The last time I had an even semi-serious relationship was in college, and I was so emotionally detached that I had to think about my betta fish that died three days prior to pull enough tears to act sad when he told me he'd been cheating on me.

One could say I am chronically unavailable when it comes to my emotional vulnerability.

"Sure," I say, smiling back at her. "Who am I to turn down the opportunity to watch your boyfriend root around in some old lady's innards?"

Alana made a face. "I hate when you describe things like that."

"Like what?"

"Like, with the most disgusting words you can think of." She shakes her head, but I can see the laugh she's fighting back.

"That's not true. I *could* have said that he was wrist deep in—"

Alana interrupts me by fake gagging. "You're the worst."

"And yet I'm not the one who's about to go dump a bowl of urine down the drain. Funny how life works."

Alana laughs and gives me the finger while backing away. "Screw off."

I just grin and toss one of her chips in my mouth as she walks off.

If it weren't for Alana, I don't think I would be here right now. Here, in Salida. Or maybe I wouldn't be in Colorado at all. I've always loved the cold, and I might have gone up north. Definitely would have moved to a city. Not that I resent her for it or anything, but I do sometimes wonder where I'd be now. If I'd even be a nurse still, or if I would have moved on without her to keep me in the game.

Not that I've really been in the game as of late anyway.

I sigh, sitting in silence as I turn back to the window and finish Alana's bag of white cheddar chips. I dump the package in the trash can, and then it's time to get back to work.

Just like every other day.

## Chapter Two

# VIOLET

The blizzard is, in some ways, the most beautiful thing I've ever seen. A rushing storm of powdered snow, so fine that it sparkles beneath the streetlights.

In others, it is the worst, most disgusting, criminally vile thing to ever exist. I've already changed out of my scrubs, though, and the thick coat I've bundled around my body is likely to do nothing to keep the chill off my bones the second I step outside.

And yet.

"You can't seriously be thinking about walking home," Alana says, draped across two waiting room chairs. "Just stay here."

Now that I'm faced with actually having to go out there, it sounds tempting to stay put. But I've been swearing all night that I was walking out those doors at the end of my shift, blizzard or no blizzard.

I can't back out now without looking like an idiot. So I nod and pull my gloves on my hands. "Definitely going out there," I say. "I'll be fine. My house is just down the street."

"Vi, please."

"You're worried about nothing," I promise Alana. "I'll be okay. I think I can manage to trudge two blocks home without dying of hypothermia."

"It's not the cold I'm worried about, Vi, it's the fifty mile-per-hour winds."

"I'll crouch into a ball and roll home."

She snorts, then glares and scowls.

"Not funny." Alana reaches for my hand and squeezes my fingers tightly. "If you really want to go, fine. But you call me the second you get home, alright?"

"Can't," I say, giving her a bashful smile. "My phone's been dead for the past hour. I plan to be fast asleep before it turns back on."

"You kill me, you know that?"

"You're going to be wishing you'd walked to my house, too, when you wake up every thirty minutes tonight and have a backache for the next week."

She sticks her tongue out at me. "Get out of here."

"I thought you didn't *want* me to go?"

"I swear to—?"

My laugh cuts her off. "Goodnight, Alana. Sleep well." I turn to walk away, a smile on my face.

"Your sarcasm is not appreciated!" She calls after me.

I'm laughing until the minute I step outside. And then the freezing cold blows harshly against my face and sucks the air right out of my body, immediately dismissing all notions of humor I just had. My instant reaction is to turn right back around and hightail it into the heated lobby, but I brace myself against the cold and take another step. It's a little too late to back out now, anyway. My mom always said my stubborn streak would get me in trouble.

One foot in front of the other, I make my way down the sidewalk. The streetlamps give me just enough light to keep me from walking into pitch black darkness.

And then they start flickering.

I would guess I'm about halfway between the hospital and my house when they go out completely, and I'm left in the dark with nothing but the howling wind in my ears and whirls of snow to keep me from seeing straight.

Definitely should have stayed at the hospital. I should have listened to Alana, bit the bullet, and waved my dignity goodbye. But I'm almost home, and I haven't died, so I might as well keep going. Especially since if I try to turn around, I might lose my footing against the wind and end up lost in this absolute void of darkness.

I take a few more steps into the night, and then I swear to shit the wind picks up even more. So much so that I wince, and my knees buckle as I try to hold myself up. Then it's spiraling more and more, and getting colder and colder with every sharp gust of wind.

It feels like it's *wrapping* around me. Like it's tightening around my body, like I'm not just in the storm's eye but that I *am* the eye of the storm.

It had been a joke before, when I told Alana I'd curl into a ball. But I find myself doing it, crouching down and wrapping my arms around my legs to try to keep steady.

My eyes are clenched shut tightly, and I'm not sure that I could open them if I wanted to at this point.

The wind is battering against me so forcefully, so *coldly*, that I'm starting to believe Alana's worries might come true and I'll wind up in a ditch on the outskirts of town frozen solid.

It hits me then that I truly have come to resent being at work so much that I walked home in a blizzard rather than stay there past my shift. I hate being at work more than I enjoy being safe.

And that didn't use to be me. I used to *love* my job, used to love spending every second of my shift doing what I could for the people who needed me most.

Now, it's not enough. I would rather be anywhere else than at work.

Which seems pointless to realize now that I'm standing in the middle of a snowstorm, but it's the truth. One that I've been holding in my mouth, refusing to swallow, until this very moment.

I *want* adventure. I want more than staying in this town, tending to the same people I've known since I was a baby. I want *new*. I want *exciting*. I want to finally live my life for *myself* instead of for everyone else.

Unfortunately, this revelation didn't slap me across the face until my life started flashing before my eyes, but better late than never, I guess.

With my eyes closed and my whole body braced against the wind, it takes a second for the change to register in my mind, but the second it does, my body tenses even more than before.

The wind stopped. It's still cold, obviously, and I still feel snow brushing gently against my face, but there's no wind.

Suddenly, it's gone. Faster than I could have snapped my fingers.

*Holy fuck.* Did I actually just die? Am I dead?

Because I'm pretty sure blizzards aren't just there one second and gone the next. It's more of a gradual fading, sometimes slow enough that the only way you can tell it's fading is when your house stops creaking against the brutality of the wind.

I need to open my eyes. But if I open them, I risk not seeing the snow-covered cement beneath me. It might be heaven. Would I even know heaven if I saw it? Would I know I was dead?

"What is this little thing?" A voice says, a chilling and curious voice. It sounds demeaning, almost. But more than that, it sounds... old. Masculine and clear, and not old in a way that leads me to believe it's an old man that stands there, but *ancient*.

I force myself to uncurl my arms from around my legs. To try to look less meek, less *little*. Look like more of a threat than I actually am. The chill that rattles through me wraps right around my heart the second I open my eyes and my gaze locks on a pair of icy blue eyes.

When he speaks, it's not the same voice as before. His voice is one of pure ice, of authority and power and distaste.

"She," he says, eyes darkening with hatred, "Is my mate."

The voice from before says nonchalantly, "Is she?"

Surprise adds to the curiosity from earlier, and I tear my gaze away from those blue eyes until I meet a pair of smokey gray ones. His face is all sharp lines and features that seem almost dainty in comparison.

"It would seem so," the blue-eyed one murmurs. "If the prophecy is accurate."

*Mate.* I don't know what it means, nor do I particularly care for him calling me his *anything*, but I'm more worried about looking like I'm not freaking the fuck out than I am about figuring out whatever the hell they are talking about.

I force myself to stand on shaky legs, eyes back on the one who seems to believe he has some sort of claim on me. The one with icy blue eyes and long white hair. *And is his skin blue?*

"Who are you?"

One of his brows quirks and a dangerous smile teases at his lips, though it is nowhere near an authentic one. Or comforting. It only sets me more on edge than I already was.

"Insulting that you should ask who I am after trespassing into my kingdom. You are the one who needs to explain yourself."

"I have nothing to explain." I lift my chin in defiance, even as the word *kingdom* is rattling around in my brain.

"Nothing at all? Not even as to how you find yourself in my realm?"

"Your *realm*? Listen—are you okay? I can take you back to the hospital if—" Then my eyes finally settle on something besides the two men before me and the gently cascading snow around us. Something in the distance catches my attention, making my breath catch in my throat.

A castle. Not just any castle—a massive structure that pierces the pearl-gray sky like a crown of crystalline spires. Around it sprawls a city unlike anything I've ever seen, with buildings that seem to be roofed in sheets of pristine ice, their surfaces gleaming with an otherworldly blue-white radiance.

The air here feels different too. It's crisp and sharp, carrying hints of pine and winter mint that make my nose tingle. Each breath forms a thick cloud in front of my face, and my ears pop from what must be the altitude.

The snow crunching beneath my feet isn't the wet, heavy stuff I'm used to in Colorado—it's powdery and dry, almost like diamond dust.

The entire scene before me feels impossible, like I've stepped through the pages of a fairytale. Or more accurately, ridden a damn tornado to Oz. Wherever the hell we are, it's definitely not Salida, and it's sure as hell not anywhere in Colorado I've ever seen.

"Where the fuck am I?"

"Like I said before," the white-haired man says, "this is my kingdom."

"Right," I say, forcing myself to look over at him again. "And like *I* said before, who are you?"

The silver-eyed one laughs darkly. "A bit dense, isn't she?"

A sigh from Blue Eyes. He runs a pale blue hand down the front of his old-fashioned jacket and flicks his gaze to mine, ignoring his friend entirely. "I am Jack Frost," he says simply, and I swear the icy hold on my heart only tightens. "And you need to leave."

Then he turns and walks away, the black-haired friend following behind him with nothing more than a gesture.

Leaving me standing here, alone.

In an entirely different fucking realm than the one I was in fifteen minutes ago.

## Chapter Three

# JACK

Gabriel laughs as we walk away, leaving the girl standing alone in the snow.

"I have to admit that wasn't what I thought you meant when you sensed a disturbance outside the city."

*Disturbance* had been the easiest way to describe it at the time. Now I know that what I really meant was *warmth*. It was warmth I had felt from so far away, warmth that had drawn me out of my study with nothing but a dagger and Gabriel at my side to defend myself.

Turns out there was nothing for me to defend from at all. Just a girl from the mortal realm who needs to return to it.

Immediately. Preferably before I spare even one more thought for her.

"Not what I expected, either," I mutter, fighting to keep the frost that grows on my fingertips from spreading any further.

A woman from another realm entirely. A woman who, if luck had been on my side even a bit, I never would have crossed paths with at all. But somehow, she's here. Somehow, my mate has shown up in my kingdom.

*Not your mate*, I remind myself. *Not unless we accept each other.*

Which we won't. She'll be gone before I know it, a problem that will quickly fade. Something I'll never have to worry about again.

Gabriel turns to look over his shoulder, then laughs. "Your mate is running toward us."

"Foolish girl."

"Or incredibly brave. As she would have to be, for the fates to bond her to you."

I scowl.

Behind us, the woman shouts, "Just hold on a minute! Fuck's sake." She grumbles the last part quietly enough that, were it not for the breezing wind that does my bidding, I likely wouldn't have heard.

"Long time since someone talked to you like that, yeah? Especially a girl."

How right Gabriel is. Most people do what I say and do it with a smile. Then they ask for some measly favor in return. Women commonly offer me their bodies for a night or two, hoping it will lead them to a crown.

But I do not plan on sharing my crown, my throne, and certainly not my kingdom. Especially with someone prophesied to be the ruin of all those things.

"I can't say I missed it," I lie, slowing to a stop before turning around, watching as the brown-haired woman runs toward us, cheeks flushed. Because of course I miss being spoken to like I'm a person, and not a god. I even miss arguing.

I have a feeling this woman knows how to argue.

"Go back to the castle." I turn to Gabriel. "You're no longer needed."

"Jack, I don't think—"

"—And I don't care. Leave us."

He hesitates for a long moment, jaw set with anger, but then goes, like the good little subordinate he is. Gabriel is the only one still willing to question me, though it's still my will he bends to, my orders he heeds. I can tell it grates on his nerves. He would be less qualified for the job if it didn't.

Though there are other reasons I keep him so close, it's what has persuaded me to make him my right hand. His willingness to second guess me. And while I am more right than I am wrong, he is still a safety measure that helps me ensure I make the best decisions for my kingdom.

I watch as she approaches with heavy-footed steps through the snow. Her chest rises and falls with the weight of her panting breaths.

"I don't know how I got here," she huffs.

"Then I suppose you'll have to figure it out, won't you?"

She glares at me. "You can be an ass, *Jack Frost*, and leave me out here to freeze to death, or you can help me get the hell out of your ice kingdom so I can go home just like you asked me to."

"You're asking for help."

"No." Her eyes flicker with aggravation. "I'm giving you an ultimatum: either you pull your head out of your ass and get me out of here, or I'll curl up on your doorstep and slowly freeze to death."

"That's not how it works here. The cold won't kill you."

"Fine, then. I'll just become your problem for the rest of my life."

Given that even mortals don't age past maturity here, that would be a very long time.

And I can't have that. Not considering the... bond she and I have.

The faster I get her home, the faster I can stop thinking about her. My teeth are clenched tightly together as I eye her up and down, as if the answer might be written on her body somewhere.

My eyes scan her form, finding nothing but loose pants covering up long legs, shapeless white footwear that offends my very senses, and an oversized coat with her fists jammed deep in the pockets. A peek of fabric peeks out from under the coat—the same dull shade as those baggy pants she's wearing.

She looks down at herself. "I'm a nurse. Trust me, this isn't an outfit I like to be seen in anywhere outside of the hospital." Then she pulls one hand out of her coat pocket and holds it out to me. "I'm Violet Jones."

I look at her hand with a frown before turning away. "Come on, the sooner you leave, the better."

Behind me, she scoffs. "No wonder nobody ever talks about what a charming man Jack Frost is."

"Most who meet me wind up with pneumonia. A deathly case of it."

I can't see it, but somehow I know that Violet Jones rolls her eyes. "Just as I said. *Charming*."

I sigh and glance back and forth between her and my castle, which I desperately regret leaving this morning. I should have ignored the warmth. I should have known that there is nothing good about something so meltingly soft for someone as ice cold as me.

Because this, *her*, could not possibly be good. Her being here at all, however it managed to happen, puts my entire kingdom in danger. She is a disease, a contagious one, if the prophecy is to be believed. The same prophecy that foretold of a mortal woman whose warmth would melt not just my frozen heart, but the very foundations of my realm.

I can feel it already—the way her presence makes the ice beneath my feet soften, how the perpetual frost coating my castle's walls drips in steady rivulets since she arrived. Each smile she flashes, each defiant word she hurls my way, brings another degree of devastating heat.

And the prophecies have never lied before.

They warned that love would be my undoing, that allowing myself to feel anything but cold indifference would spell doom for everything I've spent centuries protecting. My subjects. My kingdom. The delicate balance of winter itself.

But if I can get Violet Jones out of my realm before her warmth sets in, perhaps the damage she causes will be containable. Fixable. Something I can hope to reverse.

Though I'm not even sure where to begin when it comes to sending her back home. It's not the same as sending myself between realms—I am nothing more than a lifelike hologram when I visit the mortal realm. Real and not all at once, thanks to my magic. But Violet Jones does not have magic. She is merely human. Getting her home will require an entirely different sort of magic.

But it's not impossible. If it were, she never would have found herself here in the first place. It's just going to take time. Time I may not have, but will somehow need to find.

Everything else has suddenly become secondary. The only thing that matters until she's gone is figuring out *how* I'm going to make that happen.

Violet shivers, but says, "It's so beautiful here."

"I take pride in my kingdom."

She murmurs something beneath her breath, then says louder, "Clearly."

I turn to cast a look at her over my shoulder. "What was that?"

"I said 'clearly'."

"No." I shake my head. "Before that."

"Oh, nothing." She laughs lightly. "Just that this is what I get for wanting a little adventure."

Violet looks up at the sky as if it has anything to do with this. "I meant Hawaii, not an entirely different fucking planet." She narrows her gaze, then adds, "One with two moons. Beautiful sky, though. I've never seen anything quite like it. Too much pollution where I live, you know?"

"Yes," I say, nodding. "You mortals are disgusting things."

She presses a hand to her chest and pouts her lips. "That's the nicest thing you've said all day."

"It's been thirty minutes since I met you."

"Maybe, but I'd bet it'll still hold true."

A good guess on her part, but not one I'm willing to admit to.

"No need to keep talking," I say instead. "When we get to the palace, I'll have a servant take you to your room. You can rest and warm up, and I'll figure out how to get you home."

"So you're going to lock me in a room until you kick me out of your realm?"

"No."

"No?"

"No. Go wherever you'd like, so long as it's away from me."

"Well. I'm feeling more and more welcome already."

"Then it seems I'm setting the wrong tone." I don't bother looking at her as I turn down the cobbled path. The icy gates to my castle sense my magic and begin to open for me in anticipation.

Violet grumbles under her breath. "It was a joke."

"Semantics," I reply briskly. Then I turn to face Violet. "So long as we're clear on you keeping well away from me, Violet Jones, I don't particularly care what you do."

"Fine," she snaps.

"Fine."

And that is that.

## Chapter Four
# VIOLET

The second I step into the castle behind Jack Frost—*Jack Motherfucking Frost*—he snaps his fingers and a servant appears. "Take her," he says simply.

"Where?" the servant replies.

"Anywhere." Then he strides off and leaves me there, alone with one of his maids who looks just as confused about my presence as I am.

She clears her throat and says, "Well, alright. I suppose you should follow me, then?"

She says it like a question, like she's not sure I'll agree. But seeing as I have no idea what the hell is even going on, I nod and follow her as she leads me down a long hallway.

Too nonchalantly to be truly casual, she says, "I don't believe I've seen you around before, miss. Do you come from a different village?"

I can't help but laugh. "I'm from a different *planet*."

She's quiet for a long moment. "Oh. That sounds terribly lonely, if you don't mind me saying."

I realize then that she's right. I've been here an hour at most, but it is cripplingly lonely, knowing that every person I've ever known isn't even on the same plane of existence as I am right now. A cold that has nothing to do with this kingdom of ice settles into my bones, my heart.

I am alone. Trapped, and alone. I wanted adventure, yes, but this is far different from a twelve-hour plane ride. This isn't like that time I backpacked through Europe after college, where home was just a phone call away. Here, I might as well be dead to everyone I love.

I have a feeling it'll be a hell of a lot longer than that before I get back to Earth. I doubt this is the kind of easy fix Jack seems to be praying it is.

Shit, I'm praying too, and I haven't set foot in a church since I was twelve.

*Maybe I should be soaking it in*. Maybe I should think about how, even if not exactly in the way that I hoped, I did get what I wanted.

I have the adventure that I haven't been able to stop thinking about for as long as I can remember now. I don't have to trudge through work pretending that I still love my job, feeling guilty because I don't.

Maybe I'm trapped here, but maybe I should make the best of it despite that. After all, how many people get to say they've seen an actual magical ice kingdom? Even if it comes with a brooding ice king who looks at me like I'm something he scraped off his boot.

While Jack finds a way to get me out of here, I'll play the part of the tourist. Seems like I'll have nothing better to do while I'm here, anyway.

"I'm Cora." The servant sticks a hand towards me. "Perhaps while you're here, I can be your friend. Try to make you feel a little less lonely."

Gently, I meet her hand with mine and shake it. "I'm Violet," I tell her. "And I would like that very much."

"Great!" She beams. "Then, as your newfound friend, I'm hoping you won't mind me saying that you look like you could use a bath. And a change of clothes."

"Yes, please." I look down at myself with an exhausted laugh. Then I think better of it and add quickly, "You guys have warm water, right?"

Cora snorts. "Yes, we have warm water. But if you're cold, I might be able to get the alchemist to create an elixir for you. Something to keep your temperature up."

Gratitude fills me. "Really? That would be *amazing*."

She nods happily. "I'm on it."

Then Cora pulls open a door on the right side of the hallway and gestures inside. I step inside, and it takes everything in me to keep my jaw from dropping.

*You shouldn't be so impressed*, I remind myself. *You're standing in a fucking castle. In another country—another world.*

There's an intricately carved four-poster bed made of beautiful dark wood pressed against one wall, gossamer and tulle loosely stretched from each post to the other, creating beautiful waves of creamy, soft whites, like freshly fallen snow.

Matching furniture takes up space along the other walls—an armoire that sits just beside a window framed with billowing lace curtains, a desk with an oil lantern sat atop it, the wick inside black with use. A velvet couch so blue it reminds me of sinking deep into the ocean's depths. A door with wood just as dark as the furniture is on that same wall.

I step further into the room, inching backward toward where Cora pointed.

"You, Cora, are like a gift from the gods after everything that's happened."

"Hold that thought until you've tried the elixir." She wrinkles her nose. "It tastes like manure, but I'll bring something to wash away the taste."

I press my palms together in mock prayer. "Please say you've got chocolate cake."

"We wouldn't be much of a winter palace without it, even with all this unseasonable heat going on." She tugs at her collar, clearly uncomfortable in the strange warmth.

My mouth floods at the mere thought of cake. "Then I meant what I said—you're the best fucking thing that's happened to me since I got dragged into this frozen hellscape."

"Such high praise." Her lips quirk up as she backs toward the door, giving a little wave before disappearing.

I turn and practically sprint for the bathtub. A warm soak is exactly what I need to rid my bones of Jack's frigidness, which lingers with me even now.

Part of me wonders if I could use the feeling of that iciness to track him wherever he goes—and therefore use it to *avoid* him wherever he goes. Which, yes, is a wild thing to wonder—but I *swear* it feels like it's alive. It's like it stretches with the distance between us, contorts to follow us when we move. It's hard to explain, and maybe it's all in my head, but I feel it nonetheless.

I am seriously fucking hoping it *is* all in my head. Because if it's not, and I could follow Jack Frost with the ice he's coated my heart in, then I can only assume he'd be able to do the same to me. With me.

As the clawfoot tub fills with steaming water, I survey the bathroom. It's larger than my first apartment was—though it was a shitty studio just off of campus. Still, it's absolutely massive for what it is. No surprise, really, given how gargantuan this entire palace looked from the outside.

The bathroom is decorated in hues of cool blues and varying shades of white, the floor beautifully checkered with white and deep, soft gray tile. It's achingly beautiful—the sort of beauty that's nearly impossible to find in modern America. There's a large mirror leaning against the far wall, the glass tinted and speckled with age.

I stare at myself in it for a long moment, clothed in a heavy coat and scrubs. I'm so clearly out of place here. Nothing about me looks like I belong in this world—but there's something about that fact that thrills me, even as I try to deny it, to ignore how full my heart feels.

It's when I'm studying myself in the mirror, when my eyes glance over my thick coat and see the thin outline of something in my pocket, that I remember—

My phone. Quickly, with a strong hope that perhaps I might still be tethered to my world, even a little, I yank it out of my pocket and tap on the screen.

Nothing happens. Probably because it's devastatingly cracked. Even a little bent in one corner. Apparently, my fall into this world was *not* a graceful one.

With a sigh, I toss it onto the bathroom vanity before I peel my clothes off, turning the faucet off, and sinking down into the tub. I have to stifle a moan at how good the water feels against my chilled skin.

I take my time in the bath, letting my muscles lose all the tension that's wound them up so tightly, the smell of the minty soap left on the ledge of the tub filling my nostrils as I lather myself with it before moving to my hair.

Even after I'm clean, I linger long enough for the water to become cool enough for gooseflesh to erupt before draining the water and climbing out of the tub. I wrap myself in a large, sinfully soft towel and dry off, trying to keep my body from giving into the shiver that's desperately trying to fight its way out of my body.

When I'm dry enough to stop dripping water onto the tile floor, I make my way out of the bathroom and back into the bedroom.

Instantly, the smell of warm chocolate fills my nostrils. I inhale deeply, eyes immediately spotting the neatly folded pile of clothes sitting on the edge of the large bed, next to a tray with the most stunning slice of cake I've ever seen, along with a small, cloudy white glass with a cork in it.

The elixir. The one that will keep me from fighting the cold every minute I'm here. I grin and quickly stride for the bed.

I don't waste a single second before uncorking it and downing the liquid like a shot. The taste hits me instantly, and the regret hits me like a train as I'm suddenly fighting the urge to throw up whatever the fuck I just drank. Instead, I reach for the fork and stab into the chocolate cake. It's impossible to get it to my mouth fast enough.

Cora warned me it would taste bad, I suppose. Though she didn't mention it would taste like a dumpster fire of dog shit. The chocolate cake is so sweet and fudgy, so moist, so fluffy and dense all at the same time that it instantly relieves some of the ass water taste from my tongue.

I chew, swallow, and fork another bite into my mouth before sighing deeply and setting the fork down. Already I feel the warmth seeping into my bones—or maybe it's the cold seeping out.

I can also tell that frost around my heart that the little frost fucker gave to me will remain, no matter how warm the rest of me might be.

I'm grateful to see that the clothes Cora grabbed for me will be comfortable—the second this cake is gone, I'm diving under the covers and sleeping until my eyes refuse to stay closed.

The pants are a soft blue, with flowing, silky fabric and a stretchy waist. The shirt is soft white, overlaid with snowflake patterned lace. The detailing is beautiful. Far better than anything I could find anywhere on Earth. It almost seems a shame to sleep in it, but I'm too tired to do any of the tourist-ing I promised myself I'd do tonight, anyway.

I've just finished the cake and am about to peel back the covers when a knock sounds at the door. I assume it's Cora, probably back to check and make sure I've settled in okay, so I shout, "Come in!"

I turn around just in time to catch the vaguely familiar male lean against the doorframe and smile at me appreciatively, eyes running along my body. I can't tell if he's calculating what I might look like beneath them or if he's merely trying to decide what kind of problem I'll be while I'm here.

When his gray eyes finally flick up to meet mine, he cracks a grin that doesn't quite seem as welcoming as I think he means it to. "Hello," he croons. "I don't think we've properly met yet. I'm Gabriel."

## Chapter Five
# VIOLET

Gabriel sits on the couch, long legs stretched out before him and crossed at the ankles, studying me as I fight the urge to squirm from where I sit at the foot of the bed.

His expression is polite, his pale fingers laced and resting on his lower stomach. Nothing about him is directly off putting, or concerning, or anything like that.

But there is something in his eyes that sets me on edge. Not that I think he's here to murder me or anything, to take care of a problem before it—I—become one. But him being here feels more like a test than it does like an introduction. A test to see what I can do for him, or maybe Jack, or maybe their kingdom. I don't know.

I just know that I'd really rather he leave, but I'm too curious about what he's doing here in the first place to ask him to go.

*You know what they say about curiosity and cats*, I remind myself. Yet it isn't a plea for him to go away that leaves my lips.

"I'm guessing you're here to do more than just stare at me." The words come out even. Smooth. Not at all like his general presence has unnerved me.

He smiles. "Indeed. The staring is merely a bonus."

My lips flatten and the words are out before I can really think them through, or think about the fact that I'm alone with a strange man in a strange world, and I would not be missed. I would not be found.

"The staring is about to make me suffocate you with my pillow." I don't bother taking them back, even as immediate regret courses through me.

Which turns out fine enough, because Gabriel just laughs, clearly not taking me seriously.

His voice is light with amusement. "Jack told me you had a mouth on you. I thought he was being dramatic. He's not used to people doing anything more than bowing and saying whatever they must to please him."

"He was being dramatic. I didn't say anything offensive." At least I don't think I did. I don't remember most of what I said to him earlier today—probably because I was too busy trying to function past the shock of learning that I had somehow fallen into an entirely different realm, and that I was standing face to face with the famed Jack Frost. Who was, apparently, an asshole.

"No need to worry, darling Violet," Gabriel says, his voice soft as silk, light as a feather. "I'm not offended on his behalf. I am, however, entertained on my own. As Jack's advisor, I have spent a good part of my life listening to people say whatever they feel will gain his favor. I am cheered by your lack of doing the same, despite every reason you may have to do the opposite."

"So, you're here to pay me compliments. Interesting contradiction to the insults of your…"

Gabriel chuckles. "I believe your people call them kings. Here, Jack is known as a Lord." He pauses, waiting for me to speak again, but continues when all I do is stare at him blankly. "And no, I'm not here just to compliment you. Those are a bonus." He winks.

"Okay," I say slowly, raising an eyebrow. My mouth is running full speed now, my filter left at the proverbial door. "So, if you're not here to kiss my ass, could we move on to whatever it is you *are* here for?"

A bell-like laugh rings from him. "You're delightful, truly." He pauses, and when he speaks again, his voice is far less jovial and a hell of a lot more serious. "If you are not one for small talk, Violet Jones, then I will simply say it: I need your help."

I freeze, body stiff as a board for a long moment. "No, you don't." My tone is wary, but strong. Like I'm all at once disbelieving and trying to hypnotize them out of Gabriel's memory.

"I assure you I do," he replies, leaning forward, arms braced against his thighs now. "You said you are a nurse. You know how to fix things that are irreparable. I think you would be valuable here. Just as you are clearly a smart woman, if that mouth is any sign."

He smiles at his own little joke and continues on. "Listen, Violet: we need your help. Our entire realm does, really. It has been… uncharacteristically warm lately. On a minor scale, yes, but soon people will begin to notice. They will feel terror. And where there is terror, there are uprisings. We cannot have that."

He pauses for a moment before continuing. "Jack and I have been searching for the cause of this… change in temperature, but to no avail."

"Yes, it's global warming," I deadpan. "We're fighting the same thing."

Gabriel's lips flatten. "It is not man-made evil we struggle against, Violet Jones. We take care of our things even if your kind does not. No, what we're working against is a far greater pain in the ass—Magic. Likely old magic, since it's taken us so long to figure it out. Jack tolerates me searching alongside him at the best of times and throws me out at the worst of them. I am not the kind of help he's willing to accept. But you… I think you might be."

"Because who wouldn't trust the word of a woman from another planet over their advisor?"

"You are not just any woman. You are his mate. He is predisposed to trust you, even if he wishes he would not be."

*His mate*. That word again. That sense of possession behind it. I still have no idea what the fuck it means here, why they say it like it's some precious jewel. I do know that I won't be asking Gabriel about it. I'd rather ask Cora—or maybe even Jack himself. He's probably the best person to go to, if I want to know why he feels he gets to stake any sort of claim on me at all.

"More than that," Gabriel continues, "But you are accustomed to warmth. You understand it better than any of us possibly could. I think your insight would be valuable, just as I think that the heat that radiates from you must mean something."

"It means you're all frozen solid and haven't been near a warm body in decades."

Gabriel chuckles. "You think we do not know warmth, but we do." He shakes his head before I can pry further and speaks again. "I expect that your help will come at a cost. While I doubt currency will carry over when you leave us, I have something much more valuable to offer you—a bargain."

"A bargain." I repeat the word stoically. Wholly unimpressed.

"A deal, as you might say."

"I know what the word means, asshat."

An amused grin lights his lips. "Very well. I am prepared to offer you a way home. You help us cure this ever-warming realm of ours. You work with Jack to find a cure, and I will get you home the only other way I know how."

"There's already a way? Why can't we just do that now?"

His eyes flash. "Because it is not without its consequences." His tone is dark, serious, and chills me to my core. And then he shrugs a shoulder and says, "But those consequences could be worth it, if you were to save us from heat stroke."

"I was nearly hypothermic when I first got here, and you're worried about heat stroke?"

He laughs and stands, then holds his hand out to me. "Is it a bargain, Violet Jones?"

I think it through. If I do this, it won't be the vacation I imagined. It'll be more like spending hours at a time alone with the assholiest man I've ever met. It'll be exhausting and boring, and I'll probably want to throw myself off the nearest cliff at least forty times a day.

But I also raise my chances of going home. Because not only will Jack and I be scouring old texts with a possibility of finding a way out of here for me without needing Gabriel's harder, scary-sounding method to do it, but I'll also be looking for those answers he wants in case I *do* need to take the hard way out.

Not to mention learning more about the world I'm trapped in for the foreseeable future—I can hardly see how that would be a bad thing, except for the tiny little fact that I'll be doing it while sitting beside Jack Frost.

Jack Frost, who calls me his mate, despises my very presence, who has encased my heart in ice, and seemingly tethered it to him, somehow.

I help them find their answers, and perhaps get some of my own. Not to mention getting to go home, where a trip to Hawaii will *definitely* be booked after spending time in the coldest fucking world out there.

The thought of warm sand between my toes and tropical drinks with those little umbrellas makes my mouth water. And if I don't find those answers, I'm not out anything. I'm just... back at square one.

Though something deep in my gut tells me this bargain will change everything.

"A simple exchange." He stands and extends his hand, his voice smooth as silk. "Help us solve this warming crisis, work alongside Jack to find answers, and I will ensure your safe passage home. The magic of such bargains requires... discretion. What passes between us—our discussions, our methods—remains between us alone."

I eye his extended hand, that nagging feeling in my gut growing stronger. "And if I can't figure out how to help? What then?"

Gabriel's smile doesn't waver, but something flickers in his eyes. "Then we're all simply back where we started. No harm done."

The words sound reassuring enough, but something about them feels... incomplete. Still, what choice do I really have?

I meet Gabriel's gaze and stand, then slide my hand against his. His skin burns hot against mine, in contrast to the icy bond that still links me to Jack. "It's a bargain."

The moment our hands touch, magic crackles between us like static electricity, and the temperature in the room plummets.

Whatever I've just agreed to, there's no going back now.

## Chapter Six

# JACK

I slam another book shut, dust billowing into the air.

My personal library stretches endlessly around me, a maze of towering shelves and scattered texts that mock my attempts at research. The warming of my realm grows worse, yet answers elude me in this literary disaster.

I haven't properly maintained these archives since that thieving librarian sold off my precious volumes centuries ago. I've just left it to Gabriel to get me what I needed. Now I'm paying the price for my negligence—forced to wade through this chaos alone rather than risk another betrayal. The irony isn't lost on me that my fear of treachery may doom us all, as somewhere in this mess lies the key to saving my frozen kingdom from melting away into nothing.

And now there's another reason to regret not taking the steps to hire another librarian—a woman. Violet Jones, more specifically.

My foul-mouthed mate.

I dislike her merely on principle. She insists she doesn't know why she's here, doesn't know how she *got* here. I do believe her, a rarity for me—no human, especially from that magicless world, could possibly understand how to step into a new realm. She was brought here by magic, or someone or some*thing*.

But I need her to leave. The longer she stays, the more at risk my world is.

It was prophesied that her presence, that accepting her into this world, would be the ruination of it as we know it.

> *Beware the one with earth-bound soul,*
> *Who walks through winter's sacred gate.*
> *The vessel's power she'll control,*
> *And seal the kingdom's final fate.*
> *When mortal love meets ancient frost,*
> *The old ways crumble into dust.*
> *What ages built shall then be lost,*
> *As power yields to mortal trust.*

I suspect that it has something to do with the temperature that rises a little more each day—and the warmth that I felt when Violet first arrived here. The warmth that led me to her, the warmth that has curled around my ice-covered heart since the moment I looked into her eyes.

Unfortunate. Unwanted.

I need her gone. Nothing good will come of her presence. Unfortunately, my will alone is not enough to send her back home. There's another way—there must be. It's implausible that Violet might slip into my world but cannot squeeze her back into hers.

I'm too lost in my thoughts, my mind split between concern over sending Violet home and scouring page after page for any mention of how to make that happen, to notice that the strange sense of unnerving heat that Violet has instilled in me has intensified.

I turn my head, eyes narrowed.

And there she is.

It is unfortunate that she must be so beautiful. Worse that she is the one thing in my life that I must deny myself, that I—

I blink, shaking my head and gritting my teeth. *Foolish bond*. Attempting to bring me nearer to her, and her to me.

"I told you to keep your distance." I force a frown of distaste on my lips. I refuse to be anything but cold to her. Nothing good can come of warmth, not in this world.

"And I was told that you needed my help."

"By who." It's not a question.

"Gabriel, of course."

I still for a moment, letting that sink in. Gabriel. I scowl and turn away from Violet, pretending to read while I try to process that. What game is he playing at? My advisor, while he always does what he believes is best, has this keen ability to anger me in ways no one else has managed before.

He has the realm's best interest at heart, yes, but his faults lie in his ego. He sometimes forgets that his job is merely to advise me—not to act on my behalf.

"He had no right," I say stiffly. "You may go."

"Pass," Violet says simply. "Point me to the books you haven't gone through yet. We can get twice as much done that way."

*We*. That unfortunate, misguided word.

"*We* will do nothing. *You* will go find someone else to pester."

She clicks her tongue. "I mean this with as much disrespect as I can possibly muster, Mr. Jack Frost. You can fuck right off with that tone. Don't talk to me like I'm an illiterate child. Do not condescend to me just because you see me as beneath you."

"Then perhaps you should listen." My tone is terse.

"Perhaps you should ponder what you'd look like with your eyebrows shaved off and your castle melted to the ground before you treat me like a child."

I look up in time to catch her venomously sweet smile as she winks at me. "Just a suggestion."

It takes everything in me to swallow my words, to keep my tone halfway civil. "Your help, while the offer is appreciated, Violet Jones, is not needed. And if it's honesty you're looking for, it's not particularly wanted, either. I intend no disrespect with my words, but I am far more effective when operating alone. Is that clear?"

She tilts her head to the side, thinking. After a moment, she sighs. "We're being honest with each other?"

I shrug. "It would seem."

"Alright." She nods. "Then, honestly, you should know that nothing you might say will get me to walk out of this room and never return. You should know that I will be helping you look for a way out of this mess—this and your silly little kingdom warming issue. Whether it's with your permission, or with you glaring at me from across the room, I will be here."

I swallow thickly now. "Gabriel told you about the changes we've been having in temperature."

"He mentioned it."

I shake my head, palms flattened against the table beneath me as I look up at Violet. "Yet another thing he had no right sharing with you."

"You can figure out how to punish him for his insubordination later, Lord Frost. For now, I'd really like it if you pointed me to your nearest shelf of unreads."

I clench my jaw, fighting back the instinctive urge to freeze her in place. Violet stands before me with that infuriating smirk, acting as if she owns my realm already.

Her audacity both enrages and entices me.

"My personal library isn't for mortal entertainment," I say, keeping my voice level despite my rising irritation. "You've already invaded my home. Must you also demand access to my private collections?"

"Oh, come on, Frosty. What else am I supposed to do while stuck here? Count icicles?" She takes a step closer, and I catch the scent of her—warm vanilla and something uniquely *her* that makes my cock twitch traitorously. "Besides, I promise to be gentle with your precious books."

I step away before she can see how her proximity affects me.

*Gods-damned prophecy*, I think bitterly. *Why did it have to be her?*

I stare at Violet Jones for a long quiet moment. I know without a doubt in my mind that she will not be giving this up. Wanted or not, Violet will not walk out of this room without having scoured countless tomes, same as me.

I get the sense that making an enemy of Violet Jones would be disastrous—especially if she's connected to the warming crisis, as I suspect. The ancient texts speak of a woman whose magic burns brighter than the sun itself, whose very presence threatens to melt the eternal frost.

Every time she's near, I feel my powers strain and buckle, like ice giving way to spring's first thaw. The prophecy warned of this: a mortal whose fire could destroy everything I've built over centuries.

Now here she sits, defiant and determined, completely unaware that her mere existence poses an existential threat to my realm. I cannot afford to push her away, but keeping her close might prove just as dangerous.

So, I sigh and jerk my chin to one of the large carved dark oak shelves pressed against the wall, crammed with various books about various things. "Start there. Touch nothing but the books on the outer shelves."

"See? Was that so hard, blue eyes?" Her footsteps echo as she practically skips towards the shelves. The sound of her footsteps echoes through the library, a rhythmic reminder of her presence that sets my teeth on edge.

But as I watch her bounce away, my eyes are drawn to the sway of her hips despite my best efforts to remain stoic. My fingers clench at my sides as I fight the urge to follow her, to ensure she doesn't get into trouble. Or worse—to pin her against those shelves and claim what my body insists belongs to me.

*No. She is not mine to take.*

The prophecy looms in my mind, a constant shadow over any wayward thoughts I might entertain about her. Yet the pull remains, growing stronger with each passing moment she spends in my realm.

I turn away from where she disappeared, forcing myself to focus on the task at hand rather than the lingering scent of her perfume in the air.

*Distance. I must maintain distance.*

But even as I think it, I know it will become harder with each passing day.

## Chapter Seven
# VIOLET

I spend nearly every moment of daylight curled up in the library with a book in my hands.

There are times when I am there, and Jack is not. Mostly, he tends to his kingdom in the early hours of the day and arrives, looking weary and restless at the same time, sometime after dinner.

Mostly we don't speak. Jack never seems too keen on talking, which is fine—it's probably best to keep my distance, anyway.

While I doubt he's the kind of guy I might find myself missing when all of this is over, it's better to avoid creating any sorts of attachments at all. I don't want to miss anyone when it's time for me to go back home.

Anyone but Cora, that is. She and I have developed a routine—the second the first moon goes down and she's no longer on duty, she comes to my room where we gossip—she tells me about what the other staff members get up to when Jack's back is turned and I listen, or talk about who we are and who we used to be.

Then, when she leaves, I slip under the covers and am almost immediately asleep. There's something so tiring about spending nearly every waking hour drowning myself in little unimportant facts about Jack's realm, about collecting lore like children do with rocks.

When I wake up, I do it all over again.

Today though, as I study Jack after finishing a particularly boring chapter that I most definitely deserve a break after reading, the quiet begins to eat at me. I don't normally mind it. Some days I even prefer it.

This is not one of those days.

"How is it going over there?" I ask him. "Anything good."

He merely sighs in response.

"Is that right? It's so good you can't even spare me a single word? Do spill, Lord Frost. What is it that has your attention wrapped around its finger?"

He frowns and flicks his blue-eyed gaze over to where I sit. "What is it you want, Violet?"

"I want to know why it is that you refuse to acknowledge that I am a real-life person who wishes to have real-life conversations every once in a while. Is that asking too much?"

He straightens. "No," Jack says simply. "But if it's conversation you're looking for, you'll have to find it somewhere else."

"I'm sure you're perfectly capable of talking to me like a person for a moment or two. It might even be good for you."

"Good for me?" Jack echoes.

"Good for you," I reaffirm, nodding slowly. "Crazy as it may seem, social skills are quite important for Lords to learn."

His gaze narrows almost imperceptibly. "I have social skills."

"You just choose not to use them?"

"Small talk is not currently at the forefront of my mind, strange as it may seem."

"Ah, yes," I say, nodding. "My bad, truly. I forgot men are such simple creatures that they are incapable of multitasking."

Jack huffs out an irritated breath and closes his book loudly. "Fine, then, Violet Jones. Speak. Say whatever it is you wish to say."

I beam at him. I wonder if he can see how sarcastic my expression is. "Excellent. Tell me, how was your day?"

"How was my d—" Jack cuts himself off and closes his eyes before pinching the bridge of his nose. "This is more important to you than getting back home?"

I shrug my shoulders. "Nothing wrong with taking a break, is there?"

"You seem awfully worried about *taking a break* when you're the one who insisted you be here in the first place."

Now I'm the one glaring. "I also spend nearly ten hours a day in here, reading all your shitty books with their shitty old-timey script, fuckface. So what if I want to take a moment to ask you how your day was?"

He stares at me for a long moment. Sighs. "My day was and continues to be long and unhelpful in the grand scheme of things." He pauses then, as if it's an afterthought and perhaps a way of signaling a truce, asks, "How was your day?"

"How sweet of you to ask, Jack." I bat my eyelashes at him with a shit-eating grin on my face. "It was probably one of the most boring days of my entire life—but getting the chance to speak with you has really turned that all around for me." My tone is dripping with sarcasm.

His tone is flat when he speaks. "You're the one who insisted we speak at all."

"And it's been riveting, really. But I'm hoping we might move on to more interesting topics before I jump off the balcony."

"Like?"

"Like..." I pause, debating for a long moment on whether or not I really *want* an answer or not. *Fuck it.* "What, exactly, is a mate?"

## Chapter Eight

# JACK

I stare at Violet for a long, quiet moment in time that seems to stretch on for hours. Days. Weeks. Eons.

Her lovely green eyes flash with defiance, daring me to keep my silence. The air between us crackles with unspoken words and barely contained frustration. My jaw clenches as I struggle against the urge to tell her everything—about the prophecy, about what she means to me, about why I must keep my distance.

Really, it's likely only mere seconds before she urges, "Well? Spit it out."

I frown at her and turn away to look out the window, my shoulders rigid with tension. The words taste bitter on my tongue. "It's not important. You don't need to worry about it."

My chest tightens at the lie. Of course it's important. She's the most important thing in my entire frozen realm, and that terrifies me more than I can admit. But I can't tell her. I won't risk the consequences of what knowing the truth might bring.

The temperature drops several degrees around us as my control slips. Ice crystals form on the nearby furniture, spreading in delicate patterns that mirror my growing frustration. I can feel her eyes boring into my back, demanding answers I'm not prepared to give.

"Excuse the fuck out of me, Jack Frost, but if you're going to go around with that stick up your ass calling me *your* anything, then I damn well deserve to know what it means."

My lips curl with distaste. "Your mouth is filthy."

"You don't know the half of it."

I know she can't possibly mean it how I take it—Violet is referring to all the foul words and phrases she conjures up like a necromancer would a corpse.

And yet I imagine her on her knees before me, her mouth open wide, jaw nearly unhinged as she tries to handle all of me so that not a single depraved thing might leave her mouth—including my cock.

Then I'm myself once more, remembering my place and hers and everything at stake, every little reason why fisting my hand in her hair and showing her the true meaning of a dirty mouth is the worst possible thing for my realm.

Though my imagination does have me wondering if it's worth it, to tempt fate in such a way.

Not that I would. Not that I'd ever risk my realm for any mortal woman, much less the mate who is prophesied to ruin the kingdom I have spent my lifetime nurturing.

Violet is a summer storm.

I need to ice her out.

I turn back to her stiffly and straighten the lapels of the suit jacket I'm wearing. "I've had enough of you for today," I say, voice hard. I head for the door without looking back.

"Where are you going?" she calls after me.

I pause, hands coiling into fists. *None of your business*, I want to snap. But I suspect she'd find a way to argue with me over that, which is exactly what I'm trying to get away from. Instead, I fight the urge to look over my shoulder as I mutter, "Away from you."

I slip out of the library before she can summon a worthwhile response.

---

I stalk through the castle halls, my footsteps echoing against the crystalline floors. The temperature drops with each step, frost spreading in intricate patterns beneath my feet. My jaw clenches as memories surface, unbidden and unwanted.

*The ancient scroll had crumbled at the edges as I unrolled it in my private chambers almost 3 decades ago. Gabriel stood beside me, his silver eyes gleaming as we read the prophecy together again.*

*"Beware the one with earth-bound soul,*
*Who walks through winter's sacred gate.*

*The vessel's power she'll control,
And seal the kingdom's final fate."*

*My fingers had traced the words, ice spreading across the parchment. "What does it mean?"*

*"It speaks of your mate, my lord," Gabriel said. "A mortal woman who will bring destruction to our realm."*

I pause at a window, staring out at the twin moons hanging low in the sky. The memory weighs heavy on my chest, like a block of ice that refuses to melt.

*That same night, I'd witnessed the first signs. The great ice fountain in the courtyard began to crack, spider-web fissures spreading through its surface.*

*"It's beginning," Gabriel warned. "The mere existence of your mate threatens our realm. When she arrives, her presence will accelerate the warming. The prophecy is clear—she will be our undoing."*

My hand presses against the cold window pane. Violet's face reflects in the glass, though she isn't here. Those flashing green eyes that challenge me at every turn, that mouth that spews defiance with every breath. How can someone so small pose such a threat?

*The fountain had shattered that night, sending shards of ice across the courtyard. I'd spent the next decade reinforcing the magical barriers around our realm, desperately trying to prevent the prophecy from coming true.*

*But she still found her way in.*

I turn away from the window, ice crackling beneath my feet. The memory of the fountain's destruction plays on repeat in my mind. It was the first sign, but not the last. Every year, the temperatures in my realm climb just a fraction higher. The ice grows just a bit thinner. And now that Violet's here...

My fist connects with the wall, sending a spray of frost across the surface. I can't let her destroy everything I've built, everything I've protected. No matter how much my body aches to be near her, no matter how her defiance makes something warm stir in my chest.

I have to remember the prophecy. Remember my duty. Remember the crack of ice and the spray of frozen shards across the courtyard that night.

I have to keep her away from me, even if it kills me to do so.

---

I've only just poured a glass of whiskey and settled into the lounge chair in my office when Gabriel finds me.

"Stopped by the library looking for you," he says nonchalantly. "Violet sends her regards."

"I'm sure she does," I mutter.

"Fair enough," Gabriel laughs. "She actually sends a 'big fuck you' and plenty of other curses I'd rather not repeat. A colorful girl, isn't she?"

"Tell me, advisor, how wrong would it be to lock her in her room until I find a way to get her out of here?"

"It's borderline kidnapping at best, I'm afraid. Not worth the scandal."

Debatable.

I sigh and lean back in my chair, eyes closed as I run a finger over the rim of my glass. "I assume you're here because you want something."

"Not quite. I merely had a suggestion."

I open one eye, looking at Gabriel carefully. "What?"

"Perhaps it's useless to try, but what if you simply... attempted to take Violet back home?"

"That's been the plan all along, Gabriel. I do not wish to *keep* her."

"No, no." He waves a hand in the air. "I meant to try to shift her through the realms with you. See if it's possible to take her."

"It likely isn't."

"But you don't know for sure, right? Which means it's worth a shot?"

I hesitate for a long moment. "Yes," I say finally, opening my other eye and leaning forward. I take a small drink from my glass before setting it on my desk. "Yes, I suppose it is worth a try."

When I stay seated, Gabriel raises an eyebrow. "Well? What are you waiting for?"

"I'm waiting for tomorrow."

He balks. "Any particular reason why? You couldn't wait to get her out of your hair two minutes ago."

"Why? Because for now, she *is* out of my hair. I just walked out of the lion's den, my advisor. I'd be a fool to go back in so soon."

He blows out a long breath, but nods. "Very well. Tomorrow, then."

"Sure."

Gabriel doesn't move.

I raise an eyebrow. "Is there something else?"

He shakes his head.

I flick my gaze from his face to the door, then back again. "Then you're dismissed. No need to linger, Advisor."

His shoulders tense, but he nods and turns, leaving without another word.

I take a sip of my whisky and my mind drifts to picture Violet, her hair cascading over her shoulders, those eyes sparkling with mischief. My cock twitches, and I shift, suddenly aware of how fucking hard I am.

I imagine her lips, soft and full, whispering my name. Her hands sliding over my chest, tracing the contours of my body. I clench my jaw, suppressing a groan as I think about what those hands could do. What *I* could do to *her*.

I want to taste her, feel her warmth, hear her moans as I touch her. I let out a slow breath, my eyes closing as the fantasy takes hold. My cock strains against my pants, begging for release. Fuck, I need to see her. Now.

I sink back into my chair, releasing the air in my lungs until they burn before breathing in again.

And I keep doing it until I stop thinking of her.

## Chapter Nine

# Violet

Jack slips into the library earlier than usual the next morning.

I wish I could still be pissed at him for being such an asshole yesterday—but hypocrisy doesn't suit me well. So instead of telling him to fuck right off, I waggle my fingers at him and wink. "Someone missed me."

"Not even a little bit," he responds coldly, but he strides toward me with his eyes locked on mine, and the frosty feeling around my heart tightens. "I'm just hoping we've found a way to get rid of you, after all."

Jack wraps an icy hand around my wrist, tugs me toward him, and suddenly—

I can't see or hear or smell or feel. I just know that I Am. I exist, I'm real, and yet I am not. I have become a version of myself that does not exist and yet has not ceased to exist either. This, I think, is what it feels like to be infinite. To be nothing at all. To be—

I heave in deep breaths as my legs give out beneath me and I fall to the ground, my body all at once sore and feeling new. I'm half-convinced that I'm about to throw up. Every one of my senses that used to feel normal has now been overwhelmed, and I wait until I settle back into my body, until being tied to one no longer feels strange.

I ask the question to the empty room, even though I know I'll get no answer.

"What in the flying *fuck* just happened?"

---

Hours.

Literal hours, ones that feel like months all on their own, pass. I've long since given up on trying to read any of the dozens of books stacked around me—I can't think of anything other than Jack. Or, more specifically, what the hell it is he did (or *tried* to do) to me earlier this morning.

And then all at once he's back. Standing in front of me like he never left, except for how disheveled he looks compared to this morning. His hair is all out of sorts, windswept every which way and sticking up in odd directions, the white spikes almost looking like they're made of icicles now that they aren't so carefully styled.

He exhales a long, exhausted-sounding breath and doesn't spare me a glance before turning and heading for the door, snow falling from his boots with each step.

"That's fine," I deadpan. It stops Jack in his tracks. "Don't acknowledge me. Don't even try to explain what you did to me earlier. Or why you were gone for four hours and don't even seem to care enough to even check to see if I am okay after that."

He lifts his head to the sky, as if exasperated. Like *he's* the one who's spent half the day waiting for him to return.

Then he turns around and looks me in the eye. "I attempted to take you with me when I went back to Earth. My hope was that I could merely drop you off and go home. It didn't work."

"It felt like I left my body."

"You likely did. Your mortal body isn't meant to travel to and from realms like mine is. Actually, it's a surprise to me you're sitting here, arguing with me like usual. I expected profuse vomiting."

"Well, you were gone a while."

"Time moves differently here."

"*That* differently? It was morning when you left. The moons are setting now."

He groans. "Fine. There were... *things* I needed to tend to on your planet."

"*Oh*? Little Jack Frost, do you have a fuck buddy?"

"A *what*? You know what—no. Don't answer that."

"It's no strings attached fucking. Or do you prefer the term *making love*, you absolute prude?" I snicker.

"*No*. No, that's enough out of you."

"And not *nearly* enough out of *you*. What's going on with Earth?"

Jack stares at me for a long moment. I can see the conflict in his eyes. The debate. He doesn't look away from me once as he decides if he's going to tell me the truth, or if he's going to tell me to fuck off.

"Do you remember when I said my realm has been getting warmer as of late?"

"Yes," I drawl. Though remembering how cold I felt when I first got here, I'm not sure how that's possible.

"*Your* realm seems to be suffering the opposite effect."

I frown. "Where'd you go?"

"I was attempting to take you home."

"So Colorado? It's winter there."

He narrows his eyes at me, the blue in them turning colder than the first frost of winter. "I am the reason for your winters. I did not give you *that*." The way he emphasizes 'that' makes my skin prickle with unease.

My heart stills in my chest, and then it picks up again in overtime, hammering against my ribs like it's trying to escape. Fuck. The implications of what he's saying hit me like an avalanche.

"The blizzard? Is it still there?" I can barely get the words out, my throat tight with fear of his answer.

"I'm very much hoping that the 'blizzard' you were foolish enough to walk into was nowhere near as bad as the one they were fighting, or I might honestly have to send you to our alchemist for intelligence testing." I open my mouth to speak, but Jack continues on. "That's why I was there for so long. I was...diffusing it, if you will."

I frown slightly. "That sounds... considerably less fun than fucking."

His pale blue skin makes it easy to note the light blush that colors his cheeks. "Quite."

Something about his boyish embarrassment is... endearing to me. Cute. So at odds with the usual harsh, regal side of him I am usually treated with.

But I clear my throat, shake my head, and force myself to focus. "So, you were in Salida then?"

"I was wherever it is you came from. I don't memorize all your made up names of carbon copies of the same cities and towns. I used my magic to try to pull you back to a familiar place and landed in a hospital full of people wearing those ugly clothes you first arrived in."

"They're *scrubs*," I reply, frowning. "They're not meant to get your dick hard."

Jack shakes his head, distaste written all over his features. "If you're done interrogating me, I'm—"

"No," I cut in. "Not yet. If you were at the hospital, does that mean you saw my friend Alana? Was she okay?" Guilt seeps into my bones. I've been so busy trying to get home that I've hardly thought about how worried Alana must be.

"I wouldn't have known her if I met her," he says, shrugging. "The whole town was chaos, however. I'm not sure any of them would have identified as 'okay.'"

*Fuck*. A cold pit forms in my stomach that has nothing to do with Jack's magic. The image of Alana trying to handle a hospital full of emergencies without me hits like a physical blow.

"Take me back." My voice comes out stronger than I expect. "Right now."

"Did you miss the part where I said that did not work?" Jack runs his fingers through his messy white hair. "Your mortal form seems unable to handle the transition."

I push up from my chair, slamming my hands on the desk. "I don't care if it makes me puke my guts out. My best friend is dealing with a crisis alone because I was stupid enough to walk into your magical blizzard."

"It's not just about vomiting. If I try any harder, you could *die*."

"Then figure out another way! You're supposed to be this all-powerful winter king, aren't you?" My voice cracks. "There has to be something."

Jack's expression hardens. "Your friend is one person. My entire realm is at stake."

"She's not just one person to me." The tears building in my eyes make me even angrier. "Alana's been there for me through everything. When my dad died, when I almost quit nursing school, every single time I needed someone."

"And now she needs me," I add quietly. "I can't just sit here in your fancy castle reading books while she's struggling."

Jack turns away, his shoulders rigid. "The warming of my realm seems to be connected to the winter weather in yours. If we don't solve that first—"

"Then help me solve it faster!" I grab one of the ancient books and wave it at his back. I'm very tempted to chuck it at his head. "Stop avoiding me and actually work with me. The sooner we figure this out, the sooner I can go make sure my friend is okay."

He remains silent, but I catch the slight drop in his shoulders. *Finally*, a crack in his icy armor.

## Chapter Ten

# JACK

The library's silence weighs heavy, and Violet's earlier words about Alana echo in my mind. I close the tome before me with a decisive thud.

"Perhaps we should take a break from the research." The words in the air between us before I fully consider them. *What am I doing?* "A change of scenery might help us think more clearly."

Violet's head snaps up, her soft green eyes narrowing with suspicion. "You want to take a break? You?"

"Is that so difficult to believe?"

"Considering you've been treating these books like they hold the secrets to the universe? Yes."

I stand, adjusting my jacket. "The kingdom holds more than just this library. There are places…" *Places I've wanted to show you.* I cut off that thought quickly. "Places that might spark different ideas about the warming."

"Fine." She stretches, and I force my gaze away from the sliver of skin exposed at her waist. "Lead the way, Your Frostiness."

We walk through the crystalline corridors, and I guide her toward the eastern gates. The guards bow as we pass, their armor glinting in the light of the twin moons.

"Holy shit." Violet stops dead in her tracks as we enter the Winter Gardens, the dress Cora selected swirling around her feet.

Ice flowers bloom in impossible formations, their petals catching and refracting moonlight in rainbow patterns across the snow.

A group of frost pixies dart between the crystal blooms, leaving trails of sparkling dust in their wake.

The sight of her there—draped in winter blues and whites, fur trim framing her shoulders like fresh snow—makes my chest ache.

She looks like she stepped out of an ancient painting of our realm's golden age, when winter Ladies still ruled beside their Lords. I clench my fist, frost coating my knuckles. Such thoughts are a luxury I cannot afford, no matter how the silver accents of her gown mirror the starlight above.

"The gardens have existed since the beginning of the realm." *Since before I was cursed with this crown.* "The pixies tend to them."

One particularly bold pixie zooms up to Violet's face, its tiny features scrunched in curiosity. To my surprise, Violet doesn't flinch. She laughs instead, the sound warming something deep in my chest that I thought long frozen.

"They're beautiful," she whispers, watching as the pixie rejoins its companions.

I lead her deeper into the gardens, past the singing ice fountains where water flows upward in defiance of gravity, frozen in mid-arc. An aurora serpent glides overhead, its ethereal body rippling with colors that paint the snow beneath us.

"Jack, this is…" Violet's voice trails off as she spins slowly, taking in the otherworldly beauty of my realm. For a moment, I see it through her eyes—not as the prison it's become, but as the magical place it truly is.

"There's more," I find myself saying. *I should stop this. Distance is safer.* But I can't seem to halt the words. "Would you like to see the Crystal Falls?"

Her eyes light up at my offer, and something warm shifts in my chest. *This is dangerous.* Yet I can't bring myself to retract the invitation.

"Lead on, Lord Frost." She gestures ahead with an exaggerated bow, but her smile holds genuine warmth.

"The Crystal Falls lie beyond the castle grounds," I say, extending my hand. "We'll need to travel there directly."

Violet eyes my outstretched palm suspiciously. "What, like teleporting?"

"Something like that." I keep my voice neutral, though her skepticism amuses me. "It won't feel like our attempt to cross realms. This is a simple displacement—like stepping through a doorway."

She stares at my hand for a long moment before placing her warm palm against mine. The contact sends an unwelcome spark through my entire body.

"Just don't let go," I say as I draw her closer. The world blurs into crystalline fragments around us, reforming almost instantly. We materialize at the base of the Crystal Falls, and Violet staggers, her free hand clutching my jacket.

"Son of a bitch," she breathes, steadying herself. Then she catches sight of the falls, and her grip on my jacket tightens. "Oh, my god."

I release her hand, ignoring how empty my palm feels without her warmth. We're far beyond the castle's protective barriers now, but I tell myself the unease I feel is merely from the transportation.

The Crystal Falls cascade down from impossibly high cliffs, the water freezing mid-fall into intricate patterns before thawing again at the bottom. Rainbow lights dance through the ice formations, creating an ever-changing display.

But it's not the falls that draw my attention. It's the way Violet's eyes track the movement of the water, her nurse's mind clearly at work.

"The water here... it's different." She steps closer to the pool at the base. "The way it moves, it's almost like—"

"Blood flow?"

She whirls to face me, surprise evident in her features. "You know about circulatory systems?"

I wave my hand, and a section of the falling water freezes into an intricate replica of human vasculature. "I've studied mortal anatomy extensively. It helps me understand how cold affects your kind."

"This is incredible." She moves around the ice formation, her fingers hovering just above the surface. "The branching patterns, the way the smaller vessels divide... it's perfect."

*Stop. Step back. Don't—*

"I have something for you." The words escape before I can catch them. I reach into my jacket and withdraw a leather-bound journal, its cover embossed with intertwining patterns of blood vessels and snowflakes. "I noticed you sketching anatomical diagrams in the margins of your research notes."

Violet takes the journal with trembling hands. When she opens it, her breath catches. Each page contains detailed illustrations of human anatomy rendered in frost, the diagrams shifting and flowing like living things.

"You can add your own observations. The frost will respond to your touch." *Why am I giving her this? Why am I letting her closer?*

Her fingers trace one pattern, and the frost swirls beneath her touch, reforming into a new configuration. A smile breaks across her face, bright enough to rival the auroras above us.

"Thank you," she whispers, clutching the journal to her chest. "This is... no one's ever understood this part of me before."

The warmth in my chest threatens to crack the ice I've carefully maintained for centuries. I take a step back, but I can't look away from the joy in her eyes, which pierces straight through my defenses. Her fingers continue tracing the frost patterns, and instead I find myself stepping closer, drawn by her wonder. The scent of her—vanilla and something uniquely *her*—fills my senses.

"The anatomical patterns," I say, my voice rougher than intended. "They're based on ancient texts from when magic and medicine were one discipline."

Violet looks up, and I realize how close we are. Her breath catches, forming a small cloud in the cold air between us. The moonlight catches in her eyes, turning them to liquid emeralds.

*Step back. Turn away. Remember the prophecy.*

But I don't move. Neither does she.

"Jack..." Her voice is barely a whisper. My name on her lips like that ignites something fierce inside me, a sensation I haven't felt in centuries.

I reach out, brushing a strand of hair from her face. Frost crystals form where my fingers graze her skin, then melt instantly from her warmth. She leans into my touch, ever so slightly.

*This is madness. She'll destroy everything.*

Yet I find myself leaning down, drawn to her like a compass finding true north. Her eyes flutter closed.

"Fuck." Violet jerks back suddenly, clutching the journal tighter. "Fuckity, fuck, *fuck*."

The moment shatters. I straighten, forcing my expression neutral despite the riot of emotions beneath my skin.

"Eloquent as always."

"Shut up." She runs a hand through her hair, pacing. "I can't... Alana's out there somewhere in that blizzard you mentioned. My whole town's in chaos, and I'm here almost kissing the damn Winter King like some fucking fairy-tale princess."

The mention of her friend sobers me instantly. "The storm is unnatural."

"No shit." She whirls to face me. "You said you didn't cause it. So who did?"

"That's what concerns me." I gesture to a nearby bench, carved from pure ice. "There are very few beings with power over winter, and none should be able to affect your realm so directly."

Violet sits, her leg bouncing with nervous energy. "Could it be connected to the warming here?"

"Perhaps." I remain standing, needing the distance. "Both events are unprecedented."

"I need to get back." She looks up at me, determination replacing the earlier vulnerability. "Even temporarily. Just long enough to make sure Alana's safe."

"It's not that simple—"

"Make it simple." The fire in her eyes could melt glaciers. "You got there. Figure out how to take me with you."

"And risk killing you in the process?" The ice beneath my feet crackles with my rising anger. "The last attempt nearly tore you apart."

"Then we keep looking." She stands, squaring her shoulders. "There has to be something in those books. Some way to—"

Her voice catches, and I see the exhaustion she's been hiding beneath her stubborn facade. Dark circles rim her eyes, and the worry for her friend weighs heavily on her shoulders. She's been pushing herself too hard, refusing to acknowledge her own limits.

"We'll return to the library," I concede, knowing she won't back down. The determination in her eyes reminds me why she's lasted this long in my realm. "But first, you need rest. Your body can't sustain this pace forever."

"I'm fine," she insists, but her arms wrap around herself, betraying her discomfort. "I'm getting cold though. Let's walk. Show me more. The movement will warm me up, and I need time to think."

## Chapter Eleven
# VIOLET

My legs ache from all the walking we've done today. Jack's tour of his realm has been breathtaking—from the crystal gardens where flowers bloom in ice to the market where winter sprites trade in shimmering goods. But now the twin moons hang high in the sky, casting their silvery light across the snow.

Jack walks beside me, his posture rigid, his gaze scanning the horizon. It's like he's expecting an attack at any moment, which, given the whole 'fated mates' and 'potential ruin' situation, might not be too far off.

It's eerily beautiful, and I feel like I'm walking through a dream—a cold, confusing dream where I'm constantly torn between awe and a desperate need to get back home. I feel a sense of wonder at the world around me. It's like stepping into a fairy tale, complete with a brooding, frost-covered prince. I snort at the thought, earning a sideways glance from Jack.

"Something amusing?" His voice carries the weight of an impending storm.

I shake my head, my breath turning to mist in the frigid air. "Just thinking about how this whole situation would make for one hell of a story back home."

Jack's lips tighten, and for a moment, I think I've pushed him too far. But then he surprises me with a soft chuckle. "I suppose it would. Though I doubt anyone would believe it."

"Probably not," I agree, my heart doing a little flip at the sound of his rare laughter. It's rich, like the first ray of sun after a long winter's night.

I sneak a glance at him, his profile etched sharply against the night sky. "So, uh, you come out here often?" I ask, trying to break the silence. "Or is this a special 'show the new girl around' kind of thing?"

He spares me a brief look, his icy blue eyes piercing even in the dim light. "I patrol my kingdom regularly."

Right. Of course he does.

"We should head back now." Jack's voice carries that usual note of command.

I open my mouth to ask if we're still walking, but he extends his hand. The gesture seems almost unconscious, like he's forgotten his usual coldness toward me.

*Don't read too much into it*, I tell myself. But my heart does that stupid flutter thing, anyway.

"I can transport us directly to the castle."

"Thank fuck. My feet are killing me."

His lips twitch, fighting what might have been a smile. "Such language."

"Oh, I'm sorry. Would you prefer if I said my feet are experiencing significant discomfort, Your Frostiness?"

Before he can respond, a low growl echoes through the trees. Jack's entire demeanor shifts. His hand drops and he steps in front of me, his posture rigid.

"What was that?"

"Quiet."

The growl grows louder, multiplying into a chorus of snarls. Dark shapes emerge from between the trees, their forms liquid shadow rather than flesh. My breath catches in my throat as more materialize, their eyes glowing with an eerie purple light.

*Holy shit. Those aren't normal wolves.*

"Stay behind me," Jack orders. For once, I don't argue. I've seen enough movies to know that when the guy with supernatural powers tells you to get behind him, you do it.

The largest wolf, its shoulders reaching my chest, stalks forward. Its teeth flash—literal shards of ice in a mouth of shadows.

"Jack?" My voice comes out smaller than I mean it to.

The shadow wolves circle us. Their movements are fluid and unnatural. I count six—no, eight of them. Their bodies ripple like smoke, but their teeth gleam solid enough when they bare them.

Ice crystals form in the air around us, catching the moonlight. The temperature plummets so rapidly my teeth chatter. Jack raises his hands, and the ground beneath our feet freezes solid in expanding circles of intricate patterns.

The largest wolf lunges. Jack's arm sweeps up, and a wall of ice erupts from the ground, catching the creature mid-leap. It shatters into wisps of darkness, reforming seconds later.

"Fuck," I breathe, pressing closer to Jack's back.

Two more wolves attack from different directions. Jack spins, dragging me with him. A blast of arctic wind throws the creatures back. Ice forms around their legs, but they dissolve through it like smoke.

"They're not natural," Jack snarls. His voice has changed, taking on an otherworldly echo. Power rolls off him in waves so intense my skin prickles.

But it's the next display that steals my breath entirely. Jack's form shifts before my eyes—his already tall frame stretches impossibly higher until he towers over me at seven feet. His skin darkens to a deep, mesmerizing blue that reminds me of arctic depths. His silver hair whips wildly around his face in a wind I can't feel, and without his shirt, I can see the way his muscles ripple with barely contained power. The temperature plummets so low my lungs burn with each breath.

Two more attack from different directions. Jack spins, one hand shooting toward each wolf. Spears of ice materialize in the air, impaling them. They dissolve like smoke in the wind.

*Holy shit.*

The remaining wolves attack as one. Jack pulls me against his chest, and the world explodes in white. A dome of ice forms around us as he raises both arms to the sky.

Through the crystalline walls, I watch shadows and ice collide.

The wolves' howls turn to shrieks as Jack's power tears through them. Each blast of his magic illuminates the night, turning the shadows to nothing more than whispers in the wind.

When the last wolf falls, Jack lowers his arms. The ice dome melts away, leaving us standing in a circle of frost-covered ground. The air still crackles with his power.

My heart pounds against my ribs—not from fear, but from something else entirely as I stare at this terrifying, beautiful creature before me. His raw display of power both terrifies and captivates me—this isn't the controlled winter king I've come to know, but something far more ancient and deadly.

The forest falls silent except for my ragged breathing and the lingering hum of Jack's power in the air.

My heart pounds against my ribs as Jack turns to me. His eyes still glow with that eerie blue light, power radiating from him in waves that make the air shimmer. For the first time, I truly understand what he is—not just some magical being playing at winter, but Winter itself given form.

"Are you hurt?" Jack turns to me, his eyes still blazing with that ethereal light.

"No, I'm okay." My voice shakes. "That was... *holy shit*, Jack."

His power gradually dims, but he remains tense, scanning the treeline. His hand finds my arm, and I realize I'm trembling.

"Those weren't ordinary wolves."

"No shit. What were they?"

"Darkspawn." The word falls from his lips like a curse. "Beasts of shadow, twisted by dark magic into mockeries of natural wolves." His voice is deeper than usual. "They shouldn't be this far north."

I press closer to Jack, my eyes searching the darkness between the trees. "Why are they here?"

Jack's form shifts back to his usual height, but the intense blue of his skin remains. His chest rises and falls with each breath, still shirtless despite the freezing temperature.

"They're drawn to warmth." His gaze falls heavy on me. "To life."

*Oh.* "You mean me? I'm attracting them?"

"Your presence here..." He runs a hand through his frost-white hair. "It creates an imbalance. Like a beacon in the darkness."

"Great. So not only am I destined to destroy your kingdom, but I'm also attracting fucking darkspawn." I wrap my arms around myself. "Any other deadly creatures I should know about?"

"Many." His eyes scan the treeline again. "We need to return to the castle. Now."

"No argument here."

His jaw clenches. "Take my hand."

I place my palm against his, that same electric spark shooting through me at the contact. He tugs me closer, and my free hand lands on his upper arm. His skin feels surprisingly warm under my touch. That strange frost in my chest grows stronger, pulsing in time with my heartbeat.

"Ready?" he asks softly.

The world fractures into glittering shards around us. My body feels like it's being pulled apart and squeezed back together, every atom rearranging itself. The sensation lasts only a second before reality snaps back into focus.

We materialize in the castle's grand entrance, but my legs won't cooperate. I cling to Jack's arms, my fingers digging into his muscles.

"You can release me now." The words vibrate through his chest where I'm pressed against him.

"Fuck," I gasp, pushing away from him. My legs wobble as I try to find my balance. "That was... intense."

He turns away, magic swirling around him as the rest of his clothing materializes. "You shouldn't leave the castle without protection."

"I had protection. You were there."

"I won't always be." His words carry a weight I don't want to examine too closely.

"So what, I'm supposed to stay locked up in here?"

"Until we find a way to send you home, yes."

"I need a drink." I head toward the kitchen, knowing there's always wine available.

Jack's footsteps echo behind me. "You should rest."

"What I *need* is alcohol and answers." I grab two glasses and a bottle of ice wine. "You're joining me."

His jaw tightens. "Violet—"

"You just saved my life. The least you can do is have a drink with me."

To my surprise, he follows me to the small table near the kitchen hearth. I pour us each a generous glass, noting how his fingers brush mine when he accepts his. I watch Jack's broad shoulders tense as he stands, glass untouched. He walks to the cupboard and starts pulling out items, muttering under his breath.

"What are you doing?" I ask, taking another sip of my drink.

"You haven't eaten." His voice is gruff as he sorts through various jars and packages. "The last thing I saw you consume was those cookies this morning."

"Are you keeping track of my meals now?"

He pauses, then pulls out dried berries and what looks like honey. "I notice things. You prefer sweet over savory."

My chest feels warm, and it's not from the alcohol. The fact that he's been paying attention to what I like catches me off guard.

"Here." He sets a small wooden bowl in front of me, filled with the berries drizzled with golden honey. "This should suit your tastes."

"Thanks," I say, popping a berry into my mouth. The sweetness bursts across my tongue, better than any dried fruit I've had before. "Holy shit, these are good."

A ghost of a smile crosses his face before he sits back down, finally picking up his drink.

"So," I take a long sip, "how did you become... whatever you are?"

Jack stares into his wine. "I wasn't always Winter's vessel."

"No?"

"I was human once. A very long time ago." His voice grows distant. "There was a particularly harsh winter. My village was dying. I made a bargain with Winter itself to save them."

The wine suddenly tastes bitter. "What kind of bargain?"

"My humanity for their survival." He takes a drink. "I became this—Winter incarnate. The village lived, but I could never return. My presence would have frozen them all."

*Shit.* "That's... actually really noble."

His eyes meet mine, surprise flickering across his features. "Most find it foolish."

"Well, most people are assholes." I lean forward. "You sacrificed everything to save others. That's not foolish, that's brave."

Something shifts in his expression. "And you? What drives you to heal others?"

"My mom died when I was young. Cancer." I trace the rim of my glass. "The nurses who cared for her—they made her last days bearable. I wanted to do that for others."

"Yet you seem unhappy with your choice."

"I love nursing, but lately..." I sigh. "It feels like I'm just going through the motions. Like there should be *more*, you know?"

Jack's fingers brush mine across the table. The touch sends that now-familiar spark across my hand. "I understand the weight of duty. The loneliness it brings."

"Is that why you shut everyone out? Because you're lonely?"

He withdraws his hand. "I shut people out because it's safer."

"Safer for who?"

"Everyone." His voice carries centuries of isolation. "My power—what you saw tonight—it's dangerous. Uncontrollable sometimes."

"Bullshit." I grab his hand back. "You had enough control to protect me. To create that ice dome and transport us here."

"That's different. You're—" He stops, staring at our joined hands.

"I'm what?"

"You're my mate." The words come out barely above a whisper. "My power responds differently to you."

My heart skips. "Is that why I feel warm around you? Even though you're literally made of winter?"

His thumb traces patterns on my palm, sending an enticing mixture of warmth and chill up my arm. "Yes."

"Jack..."

His eyes meet mine, and for once, they're not cold. They burn with something that makes my breath catch.

He pulls away suddenly, standing. "This is dangerous."

"What is?"

"This." He gestures between us. "Getting close. Sharing... things."

I stand too, moving closer. "Maybe dangerous isn't always bad."

"You don't understand—"

"Then help me understand."

But he's already backing away, his walls slamming back into place. "Good night, Violet."

He disappears in a swirl of frost, leaving me alone with two half-empty wineglasses and more questions than answers.

## Chapter Twelve

# Violet

Steam rises from my tea as I stare out the library window. The twin moons hang low in the morning sky, casting an eerie glow over the snow-covered landscape.

"Finally found you. Did you sleep at all?" Cora sets a plate of pastries beside me.

"Not really." I pick at a flaky croissant. "Keep thinking about Alana. She must be worried sick."

"Your friend from home?" Cora slides into the chair across from me. "Tell me about her."

"She's... everything I'm not. Organized, level-headed, probably handling that blizzard like a champ while making sure everyone's got blankets and hot chocolate." My throat tightens. "We've been friends since we were kids. She's the only real family I have left."

"You miss her."

"Yeah." I blink back tears. "And now Jack says there's this weird storm, and I can't even check if she's okay."

Cora reaches across the table, squeezing my hand. "His Majesty will figure something out."

The library doors open, and Jack strides in, looking more disheveled than usual. His hair falls loose around his shoulders instead of its usual neat tie.

"Speaking of His Frostiness..." I raise an eyebrow at Cora.

"Leave us." Jack's command is soft but firm.

Cora squeezes my hand once more before departing. Jack takes her vacant seat, his eyes fixed on the moons outside.

"I've been thinking about what you said last night," Jack murmurs.

"Which part? The drinking or the dangerous bits?" I ask, trying to keep my tone light despite the sudden intensity in his eyes.

His lips twitch in a ghost of a smile. "About understanding," he says, holding my gaze with an almost tangible force. "You lost your mother young?"

Where is he going with this? I take a deep breath, the words tasting bitter on my tongue. "I was twelve. Cancer's a bitch."

"My sister..." Jack's voice falters, and I watch as tension ripples across his shoulders, turning them into a landscape of frozen hills beneath his shirt. "She almost died in that winter. Before I made my bargain."

"Oh." A wave of empathy washes over me, mingling with the ever-present undercurrent of attraction that seems to hum in the space where our bodies are mere inches apart. "Is that why you did it? Made the deal?"

"Partially," he admits, his fingers tracing patterns of frost on the table's surface, the intricate designs coming to life under his touch. "I wanted to save her and also save others. Though sometimes I wonder if I truly saved anyone, or if I just prolonged their suffering."

I reach across the table, my hand brushing against the back of his.

"Hey," I say softly, entwining my fingers with his, ignoring the icy spark that dances between us, a sensation that's both startling and arousing. "You gave them a chance. That's more than most people would do."

His fingers tense beneath mine, but he doesn't pull away. The contact sends electric sparks through my palm, making my heart race.

"What about your other family?" I ask, my voice gentle. "You mentioned a sister. Were there others?"

Jack's jaw tightens. His silver eyes darken like storm clouds. "She lived. So did they. That's what matters."

"But you never saw her again after…" I trail off, not wanting to say the word 'sacrifice.'

"No." The single word carries the weight of centuries of loss.

"And your father?" The temperature around us plummets several degrees. Jack yanks his hand away, frost crackling across the table's surface.

"We're done discussing this," he says, each word sharp as an icicle.

I press my lips together, fighting the urge to push harder. His reaction tells me everything I need to know about his relationship with dear old dad. Some wounds are best left frozen over.

"Okay," I say softly, watching the frost slowly recede. "I get it. Family's complicated."

His eyes lift to meet mine, and for a moment, the barriers he's so meticulously constructed seem to waver. I can see the vulnerability he tries so hard to hide, the raw pain that's as much a part of him as the frost that clings to his skin.

"Violet," he whispers, my name sounding like a plea on his lips.

I squeeze his hand, the warmth of my touch melting the frost beneath our joined fingers.

"You're not alone in this, Jack. Not anymore."

My heart's pounding like a drum in my chest, and I can feel the heat rising between us. I know he feels it too—the spark that's been building ever since we met.

It's like we're connected by some invisible thread, pulling us closer and closer together. I lick my lips, a silent invitation, and his eyes widen as he realizes what I'm offering. His breath catches, and I see the tension in his body, the struggle between his duty and his desire.

Then, finally, he gives in. Jack leans toward me, his eyes never leaving mine, and I rise to meet him. Our lips crash together in a kiss that takes my breath away. It's a clash of opposites—his cold lips and my fiery passion.

I feel the frost on his skin, a pleasant contrast to the heat of our kiss. My fingers tangle in his white hair, pulling him closer as his lips move urgently against mine. It's like we can't get enough of each other, like we're trying to consume each other.

I can taste the sweetness of our connection, a strange and beautiful mix of fire and ice.

I break away first, letting out a shaky laugh.

"Well fuck, if I'd known you could kiss like that, I might have pushed your buttons sooner."

His expression shifts between annoyance and amusement, thumb brushing over my knuckles, sending warmth through my chest despite his cold touch. "You're very... direct."

"You mean I don't sugarcoat shit?"

A genuine smile tugs at his lips. "That too."

"Life's too short for mind games. Well, maybe not your life, Mr. Immortal Winter King, but you get my point."

"I do." His smile fades. "Which is why I should tell you—"

The library doors burst open, and Gabriel sweeps in.

Gabriel's pristine white suit practically glows in the dim library light. "Your Majesty, there's an urgent matter requiring your attention."

Jack's hand withdraws from mine, leaving my skin tingling. "Not now."

"I'm afraid it can't wait." Gabriel's usual playful demeanor is gone, replaced by something more tense. "The eastern border—"

"Fine." Jack rises, his chair scraping against the floor. His jaw tightens as he looks at me. "We'll continue this conversation later."

*Like hell we will.* "No, you don't get to do that." I stand, planting my hands on the table. "You were about to tell me something important."

"Violet—"

"Don't *Violet* me. Every time we get close to actually talking about whatever this is between us, you run away."

Ice crystals form where his fingers grip the back of the chair. "I'm not running."

"Really? Because from where I'm standing, that's exactly what you're doing." I wave toward Gabriel. "Using every interruption as an excuse to avoid facing the fact that maybe you're wrong about this whole mate thing being destructive."

The temperature plummets. Gabriel takes a step back, but I hold my ground.

Jack's eyes flash that dangerous arctic blue. "You know nothing about what this bond could do."

"Because you won't tell me! All I know is that every time you let your guard down for two seconds, the world doesn't end. The kingdom doesn't collapse." I gesture between us. "Hell, when you touched my hand just now, the only thing that happened was—"

I stop, realizing what I'd felt. That warmth. That spark of... something.

Jack's expression softens, just barely. "Was what?"

"It felt right," I whisper. "Like pieces clicking into place."

The ice on his chair melts, water dripping onto the floor. He stares at the puddle, conflict written across his features.

"Your Majesty..." Gabriel's voice is gentle. "Perhaps Miss Jones has a point. The prophecy speaks of destruction, yes, but prophecies are often—"

"Enough." Jack's command lacks its usual frost. He runs a hand through his hair, disheveling it further. "I need to handle the border situation."

But he doesn't move. Instead, his gaze finds mine again, and there's something different in it. Something warmer. Like he's seeing me—really seeing me—for the first time.

"You really felt it? That connection?"

"Yeah." I swallow hard. "Did you?"

He nods once, sharp and quick, as if admitting it physically pains him.

Gabriel clears his throat. "The border…"

"Yes, yes." Jack straightens, but his eyes linger on me. "We're not finished here."

For once, I actually believe him.

## Chapter Thirteen

# JACK

*Something is different today.*

Through the window of my study, movement catches my eye. Down in the courtyard, Violet kneels beside one of the frozen fountains, her hand hovering over something at its base.

*What is she doing now?*

I materialize outside, staying in the shadows of a nearby archway. The usual pristine blanket of snow appears... softer somehow. Not melting, but transformed. Small clusters of frost flowers—delicate crystalline blooms that only form in the most precise conditions—dot the courtyard where there were none before.

My boots crunch across the snow as I investigate. The air itself feels charged, alive in a way I haven't experienced in centuries.

A flash of movement catches my eye—Violet walking among the ice sculptures, trailing her fingers along their surfaces. Wherever she touches, the ice takes on an opalescent sheen, as if responding to her presence.

My chest tightens. She hasn't noticed me yet, too absorbed in her exploration. The way she moves through my realm, it's as if... as if she belongs here. The thought sends a jolt of panic through me.

"What are you doing?" My voice comes out sharper than intended.

Violet spins around, her cheeks flushed from the cold despite the elixir's protection. "Oh! You're back. What was happening at the border?"

"Nothing of importance." I step closer, watching her face for any hint of deception. "The eastern border guards were overzealous in their reporting. A minor magical disturbance, nothing more."

Her presence here unsettles me. The way she moves through my domain with such casual defiance, as if the bitter cold means nothing. Changing things.

Even now, watching her flushed cheeks and bright eyes, I feel my carefully maintained control slipping. Each time she speaks, each movement she makes, it chips away at the walls I've built over centuries of isolation. Fucking hell, I need to maintain my distance.

"You didn't answer my question. What are you doing?"

"Looking at the sculptures. They're beautiful."

"You shouldn't touch them."

"Why not? I'm not damaging anything." She presses her palm flat against the nearest sculpture—a towering griffin. The ice beneath her hand begins to glow with a soft, pearl-like luminescence.

I stride forward and grab her wrist, pulling it away. "Stop."

"What's your problem?" She yanks free of my grip. "The ice likes it. Can't you feel it?"

*That's exactly what terrifies me.* The ice doesn't just like her presence—it's responding to her, changing in ways I've never seen before. The prophecy's words echo in my mind:

*When mortal love meets ancient frost, The old ways crumble into dust.*

"The realm is delicate. Any disruption could have catastrophic effects."

"Bullshit." She crosses her arms. "You're just scared because things aren't staying frozen and dead the way you like them."

"These changes could destabilize everything I've built."

"Or maybe they could make it better." Her eyes flash with challenge. "When was the last time you saw frost flowers bloom in your courtyard? Because I've been watching them appear every morning for the past three days."

I clench my jaw, unable to answer. Frost flowers haven't bloomed here since before I took the throne. They require a perfect balance of warmth and cold—conditions that haven't existed in my realm for centuries.

"This is exactly what the prophecy warned about." I turn away, unable to look at the way the ice seems to reach for her. "Your presence here changes things. Disrupts the natural order."

"Maybe your natural order needs disrupting."

Her words strike too close to the truth. I clench my jaw and stride away, my boots crunching against the frost-covered ground.

Let her think what she wants—she knows nothing of the delicate balance I've maintained here for centuries.

The temperature drops several degrees with each step I take, ice crystals forming in my wake. My fingers twitch with the urge to freeze something, anything, just to regain a feeling of control.

---

I storm back to my office, the image of those frost flowers burning in my mind. My footsteps echo through the empty halls as frost spreads beneath my feet, a physical manifestation of my turmoil.

The door slams behind me with enough force to rattle the windows. I cross the room and press my forehead against the cold glass, watching snowflakes dance outside.

"Troubled, Your Majesty?"

I don't turn at Gabriel's voice. "Not now."

"I saw what happened in the courtyard." His reflection appears beside mine in the window. "The frost flowers are quite beautiful."

"They shouldn't exist."

"No, they shouldn't. Just as she shouldn't be able to affect your ice." Gabriel moves to stand beside my desk.

"You remember the prophecy's warning about the mortal who walks through winter's gate?"

"Of course I remember." *The vessel's power she'll control, And seal the kingdom's final fate.*

"These changes—the frost flowers, the way the ice responds to her—they're only the beginning. Your father feared this day would come."

My hands clench into fists. "My father isn't here."

"No, but his wisdom remains. The prophecy speaks of destruction, of our old ways crumbling to dust. Every moment she stays here, her influence grows stronger."

"What would you have me do?"

"Push her away completely. Create such distance that even the mate bond cannot bridge it. Reject the bond." Gabriel's voice drops lower. "Better to wound her pride than watch our realm fall."

He shakes his head. "The warming isn't just affecting our climate—it's affecting you. Making you soft. Vulnerable."

The accusation stings because there's truth in it. Every day, I feel my resolve weakening.

"The kingdom must come first," Gabriel says. "You know this."

Something about his words feels wrong, like a splinter beneath my skin. But *I do know this.* It's the mantra I've lived by for centuries.

I push away from the window, my decision crystallizing like ice. *Better to end this now.*

"You're right." The words taste like bitter frost on my tongue. "Send for her."

Gabriel's footsteps fade down the corridor. Minutes later, Violet appears in my doorway, still flushed from the courtyard. Snow clings to her dark hair, melting slowly—a reminder of how she doesn't belong here.

"You wanted to chat?" She gives me a curious look.

I don't have time for idle conversation. The ancient words won't leave my thoughts. *She's just one woman. One life weighed against thousands.*

My jaw clenches as I force down the guilt rising in my chest. I've spent centuries building this kingdom, protecting my people. *I won't let her destroy it all.* The facade of the heartless Winter King must hold, even as something deep inside me rebels against causing her pain.

"Your presence is destroying everything." I keep my voice cold, distant. "The ice responds to you in ways that threaten the very foundation of this realm."

Her eyes narrow. "That's not—"

"You think those frost flowers are beautiful? They're a sign of decay. Of weakness." I turn my back to her, unable to watch her expression. "You're exactly what the prophecy warned about. A poison slowly corrupting my kingdom."

"Jack—"

"I won't let you ruin centuries of tradition because you stumbled into a world you don't understand." My hands grip the edge of my desk. "You are nothing more than an unfortunate accident. A mistake I intend to correct."

The silence stretches between us, heavy with unspoken words. When she finally speaks, her voice wavers.

"You don't mean that."

I force myself to continue facing her, channeling every bit of winter's cruelty into my gaze. "I do. You're not welcome here. Not in my castle, not in my realm, and certainly not in my life."

Tears freeze on her cheeks—actual ice crystals forming from her pain. Something inside me fractures at the sight, but I push through.

"The servants will move your things to the west wing. Until we find a way to send you back, stay away from me."

She takes a step backward, then another, her arms wrapping around herself like armor. Without another word, she turns and flees.

The temperature in my office plummets. Ice creeps across the walls, spreading in jagged patterns that reflect my inner turmoil. Gabriel clears his throat. He stands in the opposite doorway from the one Violet fled through.

"Well done, Your Majesty." His voice carries an odd note of satisfaction. "Sometimes cruelty is necessary to maintain order."

I glance at him, catching something unfamiliar in his expression. But before I can question it, he bows and leaves me alone with the consequences of my choice.

*This is what's best for the kingdom*, I tell myself.

But the words ring hollow, like lies whispered in the dark.

## Chapter Fourteen
# Violet

*I shouldn't be here.* My feet carry me deeper into the restricted section of the library, where Jack's warnings about dangerous magic echo in my mind.

Yet something draws me forward, a strange tug in my chest that makes my heart pound. I stumble upon a cozy nook between towering shelves of forbidden texts, the perfect hiding spot from Jack's brooding presence.

*Why does this place feel so familiar? Like it's been waiting for me?* The feeling reminds me of that electric spark whenever Jack is near, but I push that thought away. I'm not ready to examine what that means. The section appears untouched for centuries, layers of dust coating every surface except where my hands have disturbed them.

A leather-bound journal catches my attention. The cover is embossed with intricate frost patterns, similar to the ones Jack creates when he's agitated. When I open it, the pages crackle with age.

The handwriting inside is elegant but hurried, as if the writer was desperate to get their thoughts down. My breath catches as I read the first entry:

> *My son grows more powerful each day. The ice in his veins comes from my line, but his mother's warmth still lingers. I fear this combination makes him vulnerable to emotion, to weakness.*

> *The ancient prophecy speaks of one who will bring about our realm's downfall. One born of ice and fire. I cannot take the risk that Jack's humanity, inherited from his mother, could fulfill this dark portent.*

> *I must eliminate every trace of warmth within him, strip away his capacity for love and compassion. Only then can I ensure our kingdom's survival. The boy must become pure ice, or everything we've built will melt away.*

The words blur as tears threaten to spill. *What kind of monster would deliberately try to freeze the humanity out of their own child?* My fingers clench the weathered pages, fury building in my chest as I think of a young child, subjected to his father's cruel manipulation.

My heart pounds as the pieces click into place. This isn't just some boy, this is Jack. All this time, I thought he had been human before making his bargain with Winter. But this... this changes everything. He wasn't some mortal who traded his humanity—he was born into this. Born to be shaped into Winter's perfect weapon, with a father determined to strip away every trace of warmth and compassion.

*No wonder he's so fucked up about emotions.* The realization hits me like a punch to the gut. Jack never had a chance to be normal. His own father systematically tried to destroy his humanity from birth.

Bile rises in my throat as my mind conjures images of a small boy, isolated and afraid, being molded into something cold and distant. Something inhuman. My knuckles turn white as I grip the journal tighter, rage and heartbreak warring inside me.

This must be Jack's father's journal. I flip through more pages, scanning entries about magical experiments and observations of a young Jack.

> *The boy shows too much compassion. Today, he created butterflies of ice to amuse the servant children. Such frivolity cannot be allowed to continue. Winter must be absolute. Pure.*

"Fuck," I whisper, sinking to the floor. The next entry makes my blood run cold:

*I've consulted the ancient texts. There is a way to purge the warmth from his nature. The spell requires sacrifice, but for the good of the realm, I will do what must be done.*

The following pages detail a ritual. Not to protect the realm as the prophecy claims, but to strip Jack of his human mother's influence—to make him purely winter. My fingers shake as I read the final entry:

*The deed is done. My son's heart is properly frozen now. When he takes the throne, he will rule as winter should—without mercy or weakness. I've ensured any prophecy of a mate will be seen as a threat, not salvation. The realm will remain as I decree—eternally cold.*

I slam the journal shut, my mind racing. The interpretation of the prophecy wasn't a warning about me destroying the realm. It was about undoing Jack's father's magical manipulation. About restoring balance.

*This fucking asshole manipulated his own son.* The realization hits me like a punch to the gut. Everything Jack believes about himself, about mates, about ruling—it's all based on his father's twisted ideas.

Footsteps echo in the corridor outside. I quickly shove the journal into my pocket, my heart thundering against my ribs. I need time to process this, to figure out how to help Jack see the truth.

I find Cora in the kitchen, kneading bread dough with practiced movements. She spots me hovering in the doorway and waves me over with flour-covered hands.

"You look like you've seen a ghost." She gestures to a stool near the counter.

"Just doing some light reading." I pat the journal hidden in my pocket. "Hey, can I ask you something? How long have you worked here?"

"Oh, centuries." She continues working the dough, her movements rhythmic and soothing. "Why do you ask?"

"I was reading about something called the Year Without Summer. 1816?"

Her hands still. "Dark times. The mortal realm suffered terribly that year."

"What happened?"

"It was shortly before His Majesty took the throne." She glances around before lowering her voice. "The king was... struggling. His power manifested in ways we'd never seen before. The cold reached beyond our realm, affecting your world."

My stomach churns. "You mean Jack caused a global winter?"

"Not intentionally." She shapes the dough into a loaf. "He was dealing with tremendous pressure. His father had just passed, leaving him to rule alone. The isolation, the responsibility—it was too much."

*Like now*, I think. *When he's trying so hard to push me away.*

"The crops failed that year," I say. "People starved."

"His Majesty never forgave himself. It's why he's so controlled now, so careful with his power." She slides the loaf into a pan. "Though lately..."

"The blizzards back home."

"They're getting worse, aren't they?" She wipes her hands on her apron. "Just like before."

The implications hit me like an icy wave. Jack's rejection of our connection isn't just hurting us—it's affecting both realms.

"Has anyone told him?"

"Would he listen?" Her gentle smile holds a hint of sadness. "His Majesty can be rather... stubborn about certain things."

*Yeah, no shit.* I think of the journal burning a hole in my pocket, of all the ways Jack's father twisted his understanding of power and control.

"Thanks, Cora." I stand, my mind already racing with possibilities. "I think I need to do some more research."

---

I stride through the castle corridors, the journal's weight heavy in my pocket. Something about my conversation with Cora nags at me. The timing of everything seems too convenient—Gabriel's bargain, the warming realm, Jack's increasing isolation.

I pause mid-step. *Wait.*

Gabriel knew exactly where to find me that first night. He appeared moments after I settled into my room, armed with the perfect leverage to ensure my cooperation. And his suggestion about transporting me back—the attempt that left me feeling violated and sick...

*Son of a bitch.*

The pieces click together like a twisted puzzle. Gabriel's been manipulating both of us from the start. Getting me to help "save" the realm while pushing Jack toward increasingly desperate measures. That bastard knew exactly what he was doing, playing us against each other while pretending to be the helpful advisor.

My hands shake as I pull out the journal, flipping to the last entries. There, in faded ink:

*Although I am the only one who recognizes him, my eldest son's bitterness grows daily. Though born first, the prophecy speaks only of the Winter King with eyes of frost. Gabriel lacks this mark of divine right, and his rage at being passed over threatens to consume him. I fear what lengths he may go to seize power that was never meant to be his.*

"Fuck." The word echoes off the stone walls. My stomach churns as the truth hits me. Gabriel isn't just Jack's advisor—he's his brother. A brother deliberately excluded from inheriting the throne because he wasn't the one chosen by prophecy. No wonder he's been so invested in everything going wrong. He's probably been planning this revenge for centuries.

I press my palm against my forehead, trying to process it all. Every suggestion, every piece of "helpful" advice he's given... it was all calculated to drive Jack into making choices that would weaken his position. And I've been an unwitting pawn in Gabriel's twisted game of chess.

I need to tell Jack. But how? He trusts Gabriel implicitly, and I'm just the mate he's determined to reject.

Still, I have to try.

## Chapter Fifteen

# Violet

I find Jack in his study, maps of Earth spread across his desk. Crystalline markers dot various locations, but my eyes fix on the cluster over Salida. My heart clenches at the sight.

His shoulders tense at my entrance.

"The storm systems are spreading." I push through the doorway without knocking. "And I think know why."

Jack's head snaps up, frost crackling along his jawline. "You shouldn't be here."

"Your father's journal explains everything." I brandish the leather-bound book. "The warming in your realm, the storms on Earth—it's all connected to what he did to you."

"Before you tell me to leave—" I slam the journal on his desk. "Read this."

He glances at the cover, his face draining of color. "Where did you find this?"

"Forbidden section of the library. Turns out your dad was an even bigger asshole than we thought." I tap the journal. "He magically froze your heart, Jack. Everything you believe about mates, about showing emotion—it's all based on his fucked-up manipulation."

"I told you to drop this." Ice spreads from his fingers across the maps.

"Did you fucking hear me? He magically froze your heart, Jack. Made you believe emotion would destroy your power, when really—"

"Enough." His voice drops to a dangerous whisper.

"No, not enough. Gabriel is—"

Jack's fingers hover over the journal, frost spreading from his touch. "You had no right—"

"And that's not all. Gabriel—"

"Don't." Ice crystals form in the air around us. "Whatever game you're playing—"

"It's not a game!" I lean forward, bracing my hands on his desk. "Your father—"

Jack slams his hands on the desk, sending papers flying. The temperature plummets until my breath comes out in white puffs. "You dare speak of my father? After breaking into private sections of my library? After violating my trust?"

*Shit.* "I didn't break in. The door was—"

"Get rid of that journal." His eyes flash arctic blue. "Now."

"Gabriel—" I try to tell Jack about Gabriel in this moment of silence, but my throat locks up. My tongue freezes in place, refusing to form the words. *What the fuck?*

I try again, but it's like invisible hands are chopping off my voice.

Then it hits me—the bargain. That smug bastard Gabriel made me swear not to tell anyone about our deal. Fae magic binds my tongue, keeping his secrets locked inside my head whether I like it or not.

*Fucking fantastic.*

"Look, your father's the one who—" Jack's hand slams his desk, cutting off my words. My heart pounds against my ribs as his massive form looms over me.

"*Silence!*" Power rolls off him in waves, frost coating the walls. "You know nothing of my family, my realm, or me."

My chest aches. "I know you're scared. I know you're alone. And I know everything you believe about mates is based on lies."

Jack stalks around the desk, towering over me. His skin takes on that ethereal blue glow that signals his barely contained power. "Leave. Before I do something we'll both regret."

Tears freeze on my cheeks. "Jack, please—"

I gasp as my gaze drops to the swirling portal next to Jack's desk. Through the shimmering surface, I catch glimpses of my hometown—the familiar streets now covered in a thick blanket of unseasonable snow.

But something's wrong. The magic ripples, focusing on the hospital where Alana works. My best friend's face flashes across the portal's surface, her features twisted in pain as frost creeps up the hospital walls.

"Fuck." My heart hammers against my ribs. "That's why you've been watching. The ice—it's spreading there, isn't it? And Alana..." My voice cracks. The person I love most in the world is right in the path of this supernatural disaster.

I lean closer to the portal, my fingers hovering just above its surface. The magic pulses, showing me more—corridors filling with ice, patients being evacuated, and Alana trying to help while clearly suffering from the cold herself.

"You knew." I whirl to face Jack, fury and fear warring in my chest. "You knew she was in danger and you didn't tell me?"

The temperature plummets. Jack rises slowly, his eyes blazing with otherworldly power. "Get out."

"Jack, please—"

"*Get. Out.*"

"Guards!" His voice booms through the castle. Two frost giants materialize in the doorway. I back away from Jack, clutching the journal to my chest.

"Escort Miss Jones to her chambers. She is not to leave until summoned."

"Fine." My voice cracks. "Stay trapped in your father's prison. See if I care."

But I do care. And as the guards lead me away, leaving Jack alone with his maps and his isolation, I've never felt more helpless.

I pace back and forth in my room, the journal clutched tightly in my hands. The image of Alana, suffering in that hospital won't leave my mind. I can't just stay here, not when she needs me. But leaving means defying Jack, maybe even hurting him. My chest aches at the thought.

*Damn it, Violet. You can't have it both ways.*

I sink onto the bed, tracing the journal's worn cover. Jack's father did this to him, to his kingdom. All because he feared emotion, feared love. And now, Jack's pushing me away for the same reason. He thinks he's protecting his realm, but he's really just trapping himself in his father's icy prison.

*And if I leave, I'm just confirming his fears.*

But Alana... She's been there for me through everything. When my parents died, when I doubted my career, when I just needed someone to laugh with. She's my rock, my comfort, my chosen family. And she's in trouble.

"Fuck." I slam my palm against the window. Through the frosted glass, I watch snow pile up in drifts against the castle walls.

*She'd do it for me.* The thought hits hard. Alana's always been there - through med school applications, failed relationships, endless night shifts.

I stand up, resolve hardening in my gut. I have to go back. Not just for Alana, but for me. To prove to myself, and maybe to Jack, that love isn't something to fear. That it's worth fighting for, worth taking risks for.

But how? Jack's not going to just let me waltz out of here. I'll need a plan, a way to sneak back to Earth without him stopping me.

A soft knock at my door interrupts my thoughts. I tuck the journal under my pillow just as Cora slips inside, her eyes wide with concern.

"Violet, are you alright? I heard about what happened with Jack."

I sigh, running a hand through my hair. "Yeah, I'm fine. Just... trying to figure some things out."

Cora sets down the tray, her crystalline features softening. "The king has forbidden any attempts to send you back."

"I know." I sink onto my bed, clutching a pillow. "But Alana... she's the only person who's never given up on me. Even when I pushed everyone else away after my dad died." Tears freeze on my cheeks. "I can't abandon her now."

"And what of our realm? Of Jack?"

"I don't know." The weight of both worlds settles on my shoulders. "But I do know that if Alana dies because I chose to stay here solving magical politics instead of saving her, I'll never forgive myself."

She sits down next to me, her gaze searching. "You're thinking of leaving?"

I nod, not trusting myself to speak.

Cora takes my hand, squeezing it gently. "I know you care about your friend. And I know Jack's... difficult. But Violet, you're meant to be here. With him. You're changing things, changing him."

Tears sting my eyes. "You wouldn't say that if you saw how he was today. But Alana needs me, Cora. And Jack... he's so scared of what we could be. He's so scared of loving me."

She smiles sadly. "And you fear not loving him enough to stay."

Her words hit me like a punch to the gut. Because she's right. I'm terrified that if I stay, I'll lose Alana. But if I go, I'll lose Jack. And despite everything, I do care about him. More than I want to admit.

Cora shifts beside me. "Sometimes the hardest choices aren't between right and wrong."

"They're between two rights." I wipe my eyes. "Or in this case, two wrongs. Either I abandon someone I love, or I abandon an entire realm that needs help."

"And what about Jack?"

My chest aches at the thought of leaving him trapped in his father's lies, manipulated by his own brother. "He made his choice." But even as I say it, I know it's not that simple. The mate bond pulses between us and I feel the frosty pull on my heart, a constant reminder of what could be.

Leaving means giving up on fixing things with Jack. On helping his realm. Understanding whatever this mate bond really means.

I take a deep breath, steeling myself for what I have to do. "Cora, I need your help. I need to get back to Earth, just for a little while. At least until I know Alana's safe."

She studies me for a long moment, then nods. "Alright. But Violet, promise me something."

"What?"

"Promise me you'll come back. That you won't give up on him, on this realm. Promise me you'll fight for what you both deserve."

I clench my fists, drawing strength from Cora's faith in me. "I promise. But first, I need to try one more time with Jack. He needs to understand what his father and Gabriel have done."

Rising from the bed, I grab the journal and head for the door. Cora catches my arm.

"He's in a dangerous mood, Violet."

"When isn't he?" My lips quirk into a half-smile. "Besides, I'm pretty dangerous myself when someone I care about is in trouble."

The corridors feel colder than usual as I make my way back to Jack's study, frost crunching under my boots. The guards block my path, but I lift my chin.

"Move, or I'll start singing Christmas carols. And trust me, neither Jack nor you want to hear my rendition of 'Jingle Bells.'"

They exchange glances, probably remembering my earlier threats to melt the castle. The taller one steps aside.

I push open the heavy doors without knocking. Jack stands at the window, his broad shoulders rigid with tension. The portal still swirls next to his desk, showing glimpses of the hospital.

"I told you to stay in your chambers."

"Yeah, well, I've never been great at following shitty orders." I approach his desk, setting the journal down. "You're watching her suffer. Why?"

He doesn't turn around. "The magic is beyond my control."

"Bullshit." I slam my hand on his desk. "Your father's journal explains everything."

Ice crackles across the windows. "You know nothing of my father."

"I know he feared love so much he magically frosted your heart. And I know you're letting his lies destroy not just us, but your entire realm."

Jack whirls around, his eyes blazing arctic blue. "Get out."

"No." I plant my feet. "You're so scared of feeling something that you'd rather watch innocent people die than admit you might be wrong about us."

"Wrong about what?" His voice drops dangerously low. "About the prophecy that says you'll destroy everything I've built? About the warmth that's already melting my realm?"

"Wrong about love being weakness." I step closer, refusing to back down. "Your father was wrong. Gabriel is wrong. And you're wrong."

The temperature plummets, but I keep going.

"Look at that portal, Jack. Really look. That ice? It's spreading because you're fighting the mate bond, not because of it. You're so determined to be cold and alone that you're freezing everything you touch."

## Chapter Sixteen

# JACK

I watch Violet's face contort as she sees her friend through the viewing portal. The snow in her town has reached dangerous levels, and Alana struggles to make her way through the drifts. My chest tightens at Violet's obvious distress.

"I have to go back." Her voice cracks. "She needs me."

The thought of Violet leaving creates an ache deep within me that I've never experienced before. But the image of her friend fighting against the brutal winter *I* created...

"The journey between realms could kill you." My hands clench at my sides. "We tried once already."

Violet turns to me, her soft green eyes filled with determination. "I don't care. I can't stay here while she's in danger."

*She would risk death to help someone she loves.* The realization hits me like an avalanche. The words punch me in the gut. Her determination, her willingness to sacrifice—it mirrors my own choices from centuries past. I too gave up everything, my mortal life included, to protect those I cherished. Even now, I serve countless humans who will never know my name, who curse the frost I bring while remaining ignorant of how it preserves their world's delicate balance.

*I would have done the same for my sister.* The thought rises unbidden, painful and raw. Now here stands Violet, ready to risk everything for someone she loves, just as I once did.

Damn it all. We're more alike than I wanted to admit. The realization makes my chest ache, the ice in my veins stirring with an unfamiliar warmth.

This is who she truly is. She is someone who puts others before herself, who fights for what she believes in. And I've been pushing her away, treating her like a threat when she's anything but.

"There might be a way." The words leave my mouth before I can stop them. "But it will weaken me significantly."

Her eyebrows shoot up. "What do you mean?"

I step closer, fighting every instinct that screams at me to keep her here, safe. Protected. "I can create a stable portal, but it requires channeling a massive amount of power. Power that normally maintains the barriers between realms."

"Will it hurt you?"

The concern in her voice makes my chest constrict further. "Not permanently."

Violet hesitates, and I see the conflict in her eyes. Even now, worried about her friend, she's considering my wellbeing.

*I've been such a fool.*

"Do it." She squares her shoulders. "Please."

Violet's hand brushes against my arm. "Jack, wait. Those texts I found—" She bites her lip, hesitating. "There was something about a missing summer, in 1816. Your realm's magic has affected Earth before, hasn't it?"

My body goes rigid. *How does she know about that?* The memory of that devastating time floods back—my despair. How my magic had leaked into the mortal realm, bringing endless winter, even in summer months.

"The texts mentioned crop failures, widespread famine." Her voice drops lower. "Just like what's happening now in my town. Maybe there's something in those records that could help us understand how to stop it?"

I can't speak. Can't move. The parallel she's drawing is too precise, too painful. But there's no time to dwell on it now. Not when every moment we delay puts her at greater risk. If it's anything like what I faced centuries ago, Alana and the others won't stand a chance against its destructive power.

Drawing myself up to my full height, I let winter's power surge through me. My skin darkens to deep blue, clothes dissolving into swirling ice crystals that dance around my now-massive form. The temperature plummets as I gather the magic necessary to create a stable portal.

Ancient words of power tumble from my lips as I tear a hole between realms. The magic fights me, resistant to being bent to my will. My muscles strain with the effort of holding it open.

The portal stabilizes, edges crackling with frost. Through it, I can see the snow-buried streets of Salida.

Blood trickles from my nose—the price of defying the natural order. But seeing Violet's determined face, I know it's worth it.

"Go. Now." My voice booms through the chamber, otherworldly in this form. "The portal won't hold long. This will take you directly to her." My voice strains with the effort. "But Violet—"

She meets my gaze, and for once, I let her see everything I've been hiding. All the fear, the longing, the regret.

"You can come back. If you want to." *I'll find her. I'll tear down every barrier between realms if she wants me to.*

Her eyes widen at the admission, understanding its weight. I'm giving her a choice—something I should have done from the beginning.

The portal stabilizes, and I feel my power draining rapidly. Violet steps toward it, then pauses. She turns back to me one last time.

"Thank you, Jack."

Then she's gone, and I'm left with nothing but the echo of her presence and the hope that she'll return.

---

I slump in my office chair, completely exhausted from maintaining the portal. The taste of copper lingers in my mouth from the strain of the magic. But something nags at my mind, preventing me from resting.

*Violet found those records so quickly. How?*

Gabriel enters without knocking, his usual smirk in place. "Well, that was quite the display of power?"

My jaw clenches at his casual tone. "You told me there were no records of similar events in our history."

"Did I?" He examines his nails, unconcerned. "Perhaps I missed something in my research."

"You've been around the library for centuries, since the last historian left." I lean forward, studying his face. "You don't *miss* things."

His gray eyes meet mine, a flash of something dark crossing his features. "Are you questioning my loyalty, Jack?"

"I'm questioning your competence." The lie comes easily. In truth, I'm questioning far more than that. "A mortal found crucial historical information in days that you claimed didn't exist after months of searching."

Gabriel's posture stiffens. "The girl probably misunderstood what she read. Ancient texts can be... misleading."

"She mentioned 1816 in the mortal realm specifically." I watch his reaction carefully. "The Year Without Summer."

His face remains neutral, but his fingers twitch. It's a tell I've noticed over our years together. "That event was caused by a volcanic eruption. It's well documented in mortal history."

"Is it?" I stand, ice crackling beneath my feet. "Or is that what we wanted them to believe?"

Silence stretches between us, heavy with unspoken accusations. Gabriel's usual easy manner has vanished, replaced by something more calculating.

"You're tired, Jack." His voice carries a note of warning. "The portal has drained you. Perhaps we should discuss this when you're thinking more clearly."

*Jack*. He's used my name twice now, when he typically maintains formal distance. My suspicion deepens.

"Leave me." I turn away, making a show of fatigue. "I need to rest."

I hear him hesitate before his footsteps retreat. The door closes with a soft click.

Alone, I pull out the ancient journal Violet had tried to show me earlier. The one I'd dismissed without truly examining it.

*What else have I been too blind to see?*

## Chapter Seventeen
# VIOLET

The biting cold hits my face as I step through the portal, abruptly replacing the warmth of Jack's castle. Main Street Salida looks like something out of *The Day After Tomorrow*—cars buried under feet of snow, buildings encased in ice, and not a soul in sight.

I push through deep snow to get to the hospital entrance, its emergency lights casting an eerie red glow across the white landscape.

*Please let Alana be okay.*

The hospital's automatic doors are frozen shut. I yank the manual release and slip inside. The emergency generator hums, but the halls are dim, lit only by back-up lights.

"Hello?" My voice echoes through the empty corridor. "Anyone here?"

A crash sounds from the ICU wing, followed by cursing I'd recognize anywhere. I sprint down the hall, my shoes squeaking against the linoleum.

Alana stands in the supply room, surrounded by scattered supplies. Her scrubs are wrinkled, dark circles under her eyes suggesting she hasn't slept in days. She's trying to organize supplies with trembling hands.

"Alana!"

She whirls around, eyes wide. "Violet? Oh, my god!" She stumbles forward, wrapping me in a tight hug. "Where have you been? We thought—" Her voice breaks. "After you disappeared in the storm..."

"It's complicated." I pull back, noting how pale she looks. "What's happening here?"

"Everything's frozen. Roads are impassable. We're running low on supplies, and patients keep coming in with hypothermia and frostbite." She sways slightly.

I grab her arm, steadying her. "When's the last time you slept?"

"I don't—maybe two days ago? We're so short-staffed..."

"Sit down before you fall down." I guide her to a chair, checking her pulse. It races beneath my fingers, weak and uneven. "You're exhausted and probably dehydrated."

"I can't rest. There's too much—"

"You're no good to anyone if you collapse." I grab an IV kit and a bag of fluids from the scattered supplies. "Let me help you, then we'll help everyone else together."

My hands move automatically through the familiar motions—tourniquet, vein check, needle insertion. Alana doesn't even flinch.

"I missed you," she whispers, tears forming. "Everything went crazy not long after you disappeared. The weather, the accidents... it's like nature itself turned against us."

*If she only knew how right she is.* I squeeze her hand. "I'm here now. We'll figure this out."

I hook up the fluids and tuck a blanket around her shoulders. Already, some color returns to her cheeks as the hydration kicks in.

"Promise you won't disappear again?" Her voice is small, vulnerable in a way I've rarely heard from my usually confident friend.

The weight of two worlds settles on my shoulders. "I promise I'll always come back when you need me."

Alana's eyelids droop as the IV fluids continue to flow. Her breathing evens out, and I adjust the blanket around her shoulders.

"When did all this start?"

"About a week after your disappeared in the blizzard." Alana shifts in her chair. "We had a few days of calm and a chance to dig out, and then this storm came out of nowhere. First just snow, then ice coating everything. Roads froze solid. Power lines snapped."

My stomach twists. *This is because of Jack pushing me away. The prophecy wasn't about me destroying his realm—it must about what happens when he rejects our connection.*

"How many patients?"

"Lost count after forty. Mostly hypothermia, some carbon monoxide from people trying to heat their homes with grills." She rubs her temples. "We lost two yesterday."

The guilt hits me like a physical blow. *People are dying because of what's happening between me and Jack.*

"You need proper sleep, not just a power nap in a chair." I check her IV. "Where's Dr. Martinez?"

"Trapped at his house across town. Most of the staff who made it in haven't left in days."

Through the window, I watch more snow falling. The storm shows no signs of stopping, and I know it won't—not until I fix things with Jack's realm. But Alana needs me here.

*I can't abandon her again.*

"I'll take your shift." I grab a spare set of scrubs from the scattered supplies. "Let's find you an empty room so you can get some actual rest."

"Vi, you just got back from god knows where-"

"And I'm the most rested person in this building." I help her stand, steadying her when she sways. "I've got this. Trust me."

Alana's too exhausted to argue. I guide her to an empty room, making sure she's settled before heading to the nurse's station.

Time to see exactly what Jack's winter has done to my town.

The numbers on the emergency board knock the breath from my lungs.. Thirty-seven active patients. Six in critical condition. Three deaths in the past week. And that's just here.

*All because of what Jack's fucking father put in motion. And Jack wouldn't listen.*

I flip through the charts, my hands shaking. Most cases are hypothermia or injuries from ice-related accidents. The generator's keeping the most critical equipment running, but we're dangerously low on supplies.

The sound of wheels on linoleum makes me look up. Two EMTs rush past with a gurney.

"What do we have?" I fall into step beside them, scanning the patient. Elderly man, unresponsive.

"Found him in his house. No heat for three days. Core temp's way down."

I grab the warming blankets from the supply cart. "Get him to bay three. I'll start the warm saline."

My training kicks in as I work. Check vitals. Start IV. Warm fluids. Monitor cardiac rhythm. The routine is familiar, grounding.

"Violet?" One of the EMTs—Mike—stares at me. "When did you get back?"

"Just now." I adjust the flow rate on the IV. "Heard you guys needed help."

"Where were you? Search and rescue looked everywhere after—"

"It's complicated." I cut him off, focusing on the patient. "His temp's coming up. Let's get blood work started."

Mike takes the hint and backs off, but I feel his curious eyes on me as he leaves.

More patients arrive. More charts to review. More worried faces looking to me for answers I can't give.

I pause at the window between cases, watching the endless snow fall. The flakes seem to mock me, reminding me of Jack's cold eyes when he dismissed everything I'd discovered.

*If he'd just listened... if he wasn't so stubborn...*

My reflection shows dark circles forming under my eyes. I've been here six hours, but it feels like days. The adrenaline's wearing off, leaving bone-deep exhaustion.

A soft whimper draws my attention. In the hallway, a little girl clutches her mother's hand, both wrapped in emergency blankets.

"Their house lost power," the intake nurse explains. "Been walking for hours, trying to reach us."

I grab hot chocolate packets from my locker—my emergency comfort stash—and go get some hot water. The girl's eyes light up when I hand her a steaming cup.

"Thank you," her mother whispers, hands trembling around her own cup.

I squeeze her shoulder and move on to my next patient, but the image stays with me. Regular people suffering because of magical power plays they don't even know exist.

*Jack needs to see this.* The thought hits me suddenly. *Not through a viewing portal. In person. Maybe then he'd understand what his rejection is really causing.*

But would he even come? After everything he said...

A code blue alarm blares, interrupting my thoughts. I run toward the sound, pushing aside everything but the immediate need to help.

I can figure out how to fix the bigger problem later. Right now, my town needs its nurse more than she needs her destined mate.

The antiseptic hospital smell hits my nose as I push open the break room door. Alana sits at the small round table, her blonde curls pulled back in a messy bun, both hands wrapped around a steaming cup of coffee. Her scrubs are even more wrinkled from her power nap in the patient room.

"You look less like death warmed over." I plop down in the chair across from her.

"Thanks, bitch." She takes a long sip. "What the hell is going on? You disappeared during the worst blizzard in Salida history." She chuckles darkly. "Or at least it was until this one. Seriously, where have you been?"

I fidget with a loose thread on my sleeve. "Around."

"Around? That's what you're going with?" Her eyebrows shoot up. "You vanish for days, then magically reappear right when everything completely goes to shit?"

"Would you believe I was on a spiritual retreat?"

"In the middle of winter? Try again." She slides a second coffee cup toward me. "Here. Caffeine might help you come up with better bullshit."

"Thanks." I wrap my hands around the warmth, remembering the chill of Jack's touch. "I just needed some time away to clear my head."

"During a hundred year blizzard?"

"I have impeccable timing."

"You're impossible." She leans back, studying me. "Something's different about you."

*Shit*. "Sleep deprivation does wonders for the complexion."

"No, it's more than that. You seem... I don't know. Like you've seen some crazy shit."

"Working emergency during a natural disaster will do that."

"Vi, come on. We've been friends since we were kids. I know when you're hiding something."

I take a long drink of coffee to avoid her piercing stare. The familiar taste grounds me in reality after the two weeks in Jack's magical realm.

"Fine, keep your secrets." She kicks my foot under the table. "But you owe me for covering your shifts."

"I'll buy you dinner for a month."

"Make it two. And I want the fancy sushi place, not that cheap conveyor belt stuff."

"Deal." Relief floods through me. "How bad has it been here?"

"Fucking awful. Half the staff couldn't make it in. Roads have been completely blocked. We had people sleeping in the waiting room because they couldn't get home."

"Jesus."

*God, how do I even begin to explain this?* I take another sip of coffee, stalling.

Alana taps her fingers on the table. "Just spit it out. Whatever it is, can't be that bad."

"Promise not to have me committed?"

She snorts. "After the week we've had? I'd believe anything."

I lean forward, lowering my voice. "Remember all those stories about Jack Frost?"

"The winter spirit thing? Like from Rise of the Guardians?"

"He's real. And I've been in his realm."

Alana blinks at me. Her coffee cup freezes halfway to her mouth.

"You're right, I sound completely insane." I rub my temples. "But I swear I'm not making this up. He's tall, has white hair, blue skin, and can literally control ice and snow. His castle has these incredible ice gardens with flowers made of frost, and there are these magical fountains that—"

"Whoa, slow down." She sets her cup down. "Are you saying you got kidnapped by some supernatural winter king?"

"Not exactly kidnapped. More like... accidentally transported?"

"During the blizzard?"

I nod. "Remember when I said I was walking home that night?"

"The night I told you that was a stupid idea?" She crosses her arms.

"Yeah, that one. Well, turns out you were right."

Alana studies my face. "Vi, honey, are you sure you didn't hit your head? Maybe got hypothermia and hallucinated?"

"I knew you wouldn't believe me."

"Okay." She takes a deep breath. "Let's say I believe you. You spent the last few weeks hanging out with Jack Frost in some magical ice kingdom?"

"Pretty much. Though 'hanging out' isn't exactly how I'd describe it."

Her eyes narrow. "What does that mean?"

*How do I explain the whole fated mates thing without sounding even crazier?* "It's complicated."

"Girl." She kicks me under the table again. "You vanish during a freak blizzard, come back with weird marks, and tell me you've been in a magical realm with some winter spirit. And you're being sketchy as hell." She reaches across the table to squeeze my hand. "But I'm just glad you're back safe. I was worried sick about you."

Guilt twists in my stomach. "I'm sorry. I should have found a way to let you know I was okay."

"Damn right you should have." She grins. "But I'll forgive you if you tell me there was at least a hot guy involved in your mysterious disappearance."

An image of Jack in his true form flashes through my mind—tall, otherworldly, beautiful, and absolutely terrifying.

"You could say that."

## Chapter Eighteen

# JACK

I pace my office, unable to focus on anything except her absence. The space feels colder without Violet here, though that should be impossible.

*I am Winter incarnate. Cold is what I am.*

*No. I will not think of her.*

My fingers trace over the ancient tome she found, its weathered pages holding secrets about 1816—the Year Without a Summer.

Images flash through my mind of that devastating time, when my father's madness consumed him like frost spreading across glass. His obsession with expanding winter's reach threatened to freeze the entire world.

I had no choice but to confront him, to wrest control of both throne and kingdom from his icy grip.

To fight him, my winter magic had burst forth wild and untamed, like a blizzard trapped in my veins. I struggled to contain it, to shape it with purpose rather than letting it rampage.

Combined with the winter my father had already spread across the realms, the weight of responsibility crushed down on my shoulders. *Those first days of rule tested* me as I fought to control the magic that raged inside me, desperate to keep it from taking over my mind.

Bringing proper winter back, with its delicate balance of snow and stillness, nearly broke me. But failure would have meant the deaths of millions. So I persevered, learned control, became worthy of my crown through bitter determination.

*Some nights, I still hear his ravings in my dreams. The way he spoke of eternal winter, of freezing every living thing... it haunts me still.*

I slam the book shut and stride to the window. Beyond the glass, snow falls heavier than usual, the flakes larger and more aggressive. Like my thoughts, refusing to be contained.

My body burns with need, remembering how Violet's lips felt against mine, how perfectly she fit in my arms. The memory of her warmth, her softness, sends desire coursing through me. Even now, I can almost taste her, feel her pressed against me.

*Fuck.*

I put my palm against the window, frost spreading from my fingers across the glass. My cock hardens painfully as I imagine pushing her up against this very window, hiking up her dress, spreading her thighs...

This is exactly what I feared—losing control, letting emotion rule over duty. But knowing the danger doesn't stop me from wanting her. From imagining all the ways I could take her, mark her, make her mine completely.

*Mine.* The word echoes in my mind, primal and possessive. The temperature in the room plummets as my control slips further.

I need to master these urges before they master me. Before I become like my father, whose unchecked passion nearly destroyed both realms.

But gods help me, all I can think about is Violet's body against mine, her breath hot on my neck, her hands on my skin.

The sound of cracking glass jolts me back to reality. I remove my hand from the window, watching the spiderweb of fractures spread across its surface. My reflection stares back at me—eyes glowing an ethereal blue, skin taking on that darker shade that betrays my slipping control.

*Get it together.*

I turn away from the window and force myself to sit at my desk. The tome lies there, mocking me with its secrets. Gabriel's explanation about the prophecy doesn't align with what Violet found. Why would he lie? What did he know? More importantly, why did I believe him so readily?

"My Lord?" A servant's voice carries through the door. "The eastern border reports are ready for your review."

"Leave them." My voice comes out rougher than intended, and frost creeps across my desk.

*Focus on work. Duty. The realm.*

But the reports blur before my eyes, each word morphing into thoughts of her. The way she challenged me in the library. How she refused to back down when I tried to intimidate her. The soft gasp she made when I kissed her...

"Fuck this." I find it liberating, saying out loud one of those vulgar words that Violet loves so much. I had already caught myself using profanity in my thoughts.

*What else has she changed in me? How would she keep changing things?*

I stand abruptly, my chair scraping against the floor. The temperature drops further as I pace. Ice crystals form in the air around me, suspended like frozen stars. Each breath comes out as white mist, even for me.

*I should have never let her leave.*

The thought crashes through my carefully constructed walls of duty and obligation. It's selfish. Dangerous. Everything I've fought against for centuries.

But it's true.

The prophecy warned of destruction, yet everything seems to be falling apart precisely because I pushed her away.

*What if I was wrong?*

A blast of magic hits me from behind, ice shards piercing my shoulders. I stumble forward, catching myself against my desk. *What the hell?*

"You're even weaker than I expected." Gabriel's voice carries none of its usual warmth. "Sending her away really did a number on you, didn't it?"

I spin around, frost gathering at my fingertips. "What are you doing?"

"What I should have done centuries ago." Gabriel's gray eyes flash with hatred. "Father was a fool to choose you as his heir."

The word strikes like a physical blow. "*Father?*"

"Oh yes, dear brother." His lips curl into a sneer. "Didn't you ever wonder why I've stayed by your side all these years? Why I know so much about our realm's history?"

Ice spreads across the floor between us as my power responds to my rising anger. "You've been lying to me."

"I've been *waiting*." Another blast of magic, this one catching me in the chest. "Waiting for you to make the same mistake Father did—rejecting your mate for the sake of *duty*."

I slam into the bookshelf, ancient tomes clattering to the floor. My power feels sluggish, weakened.

*Fuck. He's right. Sending Violet away took away too much of my power. And since when did Gabriel have winter powers?*

"She tried to warn me about you." The realization burns through me like acid. "Every time she questioned something, you twisted it. Made me doubt her."

Gabriel laughs, the sound sharp as breaking ice. "She was annoyingly persistent about digging through those old records. Such a shame you didn't listen to her."

My chest aches at the memory of Violet's face when I dismissed her discoveries. She didn't stop trying to show me the truth, even when I pushed her away.

"You know what's truly pathetic?" Gabriel stalks closer, magic crackling around him. "She was the only one who never lied to you. Who challenged you openly instead of playing games. And you sent her away."

The truth of his words cuts deeper than any magic could. Violet had been honest from the start—about her feelings, her doubts, everything. While I listened to Gabriel's honey-coated lies.

"You're right." I push myself up, ignoring the pain. "I was a fool."

"Finally, something we agree on." Gabriel raises his hand, ice magic gathering in his palm. "Too bad it's too late to fix your mistake."

But he's wrong. The bond between Violet and me might be stretched thin by distance, but it isn't broken. I can feel it now, humming beneath my skin like a forgotten song.

*I never should have doubted her.*

The bond pulses stronger, calling to me like a beacon. Gabriel's magic crackles through the air, but I barely notice it now. All I can think about is Violet—her warmth, her strength, her unwavering honesty.

My brother launches another attack. Ice shards tear into my flesh, but the pain feels distant. Meaningless.

"You're pathetic." Gabriel's footsteps echo across the frozen floor. "Centuries of ruling this realm, and you're ready to throw it all away for some mortal?"

I close my eyes, letting memories of Violet wash over me. Her laugh when she called me 'Your Frostiness.' The fire in her eyes when she stood up to me. The softness of her lips against mine.

The truth hits me like an avalanche. All these years maintaining perfect control, protecting my kingdom—and for what? To end up alone in a frozen wasteland, manipulated by my own brother?

"Answer me!" Gabriel's magic slams into me again.

I open my eyes, meeting his gaze. "You're right about one thing. I am throwing it all away."

"What?"

"The throne. The power. All of it." A smile spreads across my face as the weight of centuries lifts from my shoulders. "Keep it."

Gabriel's expression twists with confusion. "You can't be serious."

"I've never been more serious." I push myself to my feet, ignoring the ice piercing my skin. "This kingdom means nothing without her."

"You'll lose everything—your immortality, your magic..."

"Good."

The word comes out strong and clear, surprising us both. My magic has always been a part of me, as essential as breathing. But Violet... Violet makes me feel alive in a way magic never has.

Gabriel raises his hands, frost swirling around his fingers, and hesitation flashes in his eyes. "I won't let you leave."

"You don't have a choice." I turn toward the window, toward where I can feel Violet's presence pulling at me. "I'm done letting fear rule my life."

Magic explodes behind me, but I don't look back. My brother can have his throne, his power, his precious prophecies. I choose Violet.

*I'm coming, little mate.*

The thought flows through our bond, and for the first time, I let myself embrace it fully. The connection blazes to life, filling me with warmth despite Gabriel's ice magic tearing at my back, pulling me towards Violet.

I smile, feeling more human than I have in centuries.

## Chapter Nineteen
# Violet

*Shit, shit, shit.* The storm outside the hospital windows is getting worse, not better. Alana and I huddle in the break room, watching the snow pile up against the glass. The wind howls like a living thing, and ice crystals spread across the window in familiar, beautiful patterns.

Too familiar.

My heart skips. Those aren't normal frost patterns.

The emergency lights flicker, and the whole building groans under the assault of the storm. Several nurses rush past our door, their voices urgent.

"This is insane." Alana wraps her arms around herself. "We're going to be stuck here."

The temperature plummets so fast I can see our breath. The coffee in Alana's mug starts to freeze.

"Get away from the windows." I grab her arm and pull her back just as the glass frosts over completely.

A blast of arctic wind shatters the window inward. Snow and ice swirl into the room, and through it steps a tall figure with frost-white hair and glowing blue eyes.

Jack.

He's in his true winter form—seven feet tall, blue-skinned, and radiating winter's fury. But his eyes find mine immediately, and the storm around him calms.

"Violet." His voice thunders deep in his chest like snow crashing down a mountain..

"Holy shit." Alana stumbles backward. "What the actual fuck?"

"We need to leave. Now." Jack extends his hand to me. "Gabriel has—"

"You came back." The words tumble out before I can stop them. "After everything..."

"I was wrong. About all of it." His eyes soften, even as ice continues to spread across the walls. "I need you. The realm needs you."

Alana grabs my arm. "Vi, what's happening?"

The building shudders again, and this time it's not from Jack's power. The storm outside is tearing the hospital apart.

"The patients," I say. "We can't leave them."

Jack nods, his expression grim. "I can create a barrier around the building, but not for long. My power is limited here, and maintaining it will drain me quickly."

I look at Alana, who's staring at Jack with wide eyes. "Remember when I told you where I disappeared to? This is Jack. And yes, he's really Jack Frost."

"I thought you were hallucinating from hypothermia!"

"Clearly not." I squeeze her hand. "We need to evacuate everyone to the ground floor. Jack can protect us, but we need to move fast."

Jack's presence fills the room with crackling energy as he channels his power. Ice spreads from his feet, but this ice glows with an opalescent light—the same way it did when I touched it in his realm. Our magic, working together.

"Your friend speaks truth," Jack tells Alana. "I can shield you all, but we must act quickly. This storm will destroy this building if we don't."

Alana looks between us, then straightens her shoulders. "I'll alert the staff. Ground floor cafeteria?"

I nod, and she runs out, nurse mode fully engaged.

Jack's hand finds mine, his skin no longer feeling cold to my touch. "I should have trusted you, Violet."

His words make my heart flutter, but I push the feeling down. *Now isn't the time for swooning, Jones.*

"We need to focus on getting everyone safe first." I pull my hand from his, ignoring the ache of loss. "Then we can talk about trust."

The emergency lights flicker again as we hurry down the hallway. Jack's massive form looks ridiculous against the standard hospital architecture—his head nearly brushes the ceiling tiles.

"These passages are absurdly small," he mutters, ducking under a doorframe.

"Not all of us need to be giants to get things done."

A nurse rushes past with an elderly patient in a wheelchair, doing a double-take at Jack. Her jaw drops, but she keeps moving. *Good old hospital training. When weird shit happens, just keep working.*

We reach the cafeteria to find Alana directing traffic like a pro, pointing staff and patients to different areas. She spots us and her eyes go wide again at Jack's appearance.

"Your boyfriend's looking a bit blue there, Vi."

"He's not my—"

A tremendous crash from above cuts me off. The building shakes, and several people scream. Jack raises his hands, and a shimmering dome of ice forms over the cafeteria ceiling. Through its translucent surface, I can see debris bouncing off harmlessly.

"Show-off," I mutter, but I'm impressed despite myself.

"I heard that, little mate."

Alana sidles up next to me as we help settle people. "So when you said you met someone, you didn't mention that the hot guy was the 'mythological winter deity' himself."

"Would you have believed me?"

"Fair point." She watches Jack create ice barriers around the exterior walls. "He is hot, though. You know, for being literally made of ice."

I feel my cheeks heat. "He's just here because he needs my help with something."

"Uh-huh. That's why he's looking at you like you hung the moon?"

"He's not—" But when I glance over, Jack's intense gaze is fixed on me, softening when our eyes meet.

*No. Don't read into it. He just needs me to deal with Gabriel and his realm. He called me his mate before and still pushed me away.*

The lights go out completely, plunging us into darkness. Before panic can spread, Jack waves his hand and dozens of floating ice crystals appear, casting a soft blue glow throughout the room.

"That's better," Alana says. "Very romantic lighting."

I elbow her in the ribs. "Not helping."

"What? I'm just saying, if a guy turned into a giant blue ice god and created magical barriers to save my workplace, I'd at least consider giving him a chance."

"It's complicated."

"When isn't it?" She squeezes my arm. "But complicated doesn't always mean wrong."

The building trembles beneath my feet, and Jack's protective dome groans like it might crack. His muscles bunch as he adds another coating of ice to strengthen it.

"We must go back to my realm for now. I thought I could just leave, but Gabriel wields too much power on Earth. I can tell he's trying to hurt me, but he's struggling to handle the magic surging through him. Having you near me makes me strong enough to go back and deal with that bastard."

"What about all the sick people?" I ask, glancing at the hallway that leads to the patient rooms.

"The barrier will last a few hours, at least." Jack steps toward me, his huge body blocking out some of the crystal-lit glow. "I also think they are safer without us here. Gabriel's storm will be following me, following us and feeding off my magic." He lowers his voice. "The longer we stay, the more danger they're in."

He's right, but leaving all those sick people behind makes my stomach twist with guilt.

"Last time I tried to travel between realms, it felt like my soul was being ripped apart."

"I know. I was foolish then, trying to force you away." His blue hand reaches for mine, and that familiar warmth spreads through my chest. "But I understand now. Our bond—it's not just magic. I think it's a bridge between our worlds."

Alana appears at my elbow. "The emergency response team is ten minutes out. We've got everyone stable."

"You'll handle things here?"

She nods, then pulls me into a fierce hug. "Don't disappear on me again without saying goodbye."

"I won't." *I hope.*

Jack's hand settles on my shoulder, and I feel power thrumming through him. "Are you ready?"

"No, but when has that ever fucking stopped me?"

He pulls me against his chest, and the world dissolves into swirling snow. But this time, instead of that horrible tearing sensation, I feel wrapped in warmth. Protected. Connected.

*Oh. This is what it's supposed to feel like.*

The hospital cafeteria fades away, and I catch one last glimpse of Alana's shocked face before everything goes white.

## Chapter Twenty

# Violet

The familiar chill of Jack's realm wraps around me as we materialize in his throne room. My stomach lurches, but nothing like the soul-ripping agony of before.

Jack's massive form still towers over me, but his touch remains gentle as he steadies me. "Are you alright?"

"Better than last time." I glance around the crystalline chamber.

The massive throne dominates the circular chamber, carved from ancient ice and raised on a dais of crystalline steps. Towering columns stretch toward the vaulted ceiling, where delicate icicles hang like frozen chandeliers.

Frost patterns swirl across the polished floor in intricate spirals, and tall windows arch between the columns, their panes etched with magical designs that seem to shift in the ethereal light.

The whole room glows with a soft blue radiance that makes the ice walls shimmer like opals.

"Though I'd feel even better if we had a plan for dealing with your homicidal brother."

His jaw tightens. "Gabriel will come for us here. He'll feel us arrive."

A blast of ice shatters the nearest window. I dive behind a pillar as shards spray across the floor.

"How touching." Gabriel's voice drips with disdain as he steps through the broken window. "The lord and his little whore, reunited at last."

Jack moves to shield me, but something stops him. Ice creeps up his legs, holding him in place.

"Your magic is weak, brother." Gabriel circles us slowly, his boots clicking against the frost-covered floor as he forces us away from the throne. The sound echoes off the cold walls, multiplying until it seems like we're surrounded by phantom footsteps. "All those centuries maintaining the separation between realms, when you should have been embracing the connection."

I dart between two columns, their translucent surfaces casting prismatic shadows across my skin. Jack moves in the opposite direction, drawing Gabriel's attention away from me.

"Our father was a fool." Gabriel's voice softens, losing its sharp edge. "At first, I believed him when he said bonds to mortals would destroy us. But the more I studied the prophecies, the clearer it became—denying the connection is what truly weakens us."

He runs his fingers through his dark hair, looking between Jack and me. "Look what happened to Father. His refusal to accept your Mother's love poisoned him from within. The ice took over until nothing remained but a frozen husk."

"You're wrong," Jack says, but uncertainty creeps into his voice.

"Am I?" Gabriel's gray eyes lock onto mine. "You feel it already, don't you? The way your magic surges when she's near? The prophecy never meant she would destroy you, brother. She makes you stronger. Just as your mother could have made Father stronger, if he hadn't been too proud to let her in."

My heart pounds as Gabriel's words sink in. Could he be right? Has Jack been interpreting everything backwards this whole time?

"Father was a fool who feared what he didn't understand. How do you think you were able to defeat him when you were just coming into your own magic?" Gabriel flings another ice blast.

Without thinking, I step in front of Jack. The ice hits my outstretched hand and... dissolves. Warmth floods through me, familiar yet foreign—like the heat of summer sunshine filtered through winter frost.

*What the hell?*

"Ah, there it is." Gabriel's smile turns cruel. "The truth reveals itself at last. Tell me, little nurse, haven't you ever wondered why you're so good at healing? Why your touch seems to bring life back to the dying?"

My hand tingles with residual energy. "What are you talking about?"

"You're a Soul Healer." Jack's voice is filled with wonder. "That's why the ice responds to you. Why our connection felt so natural."

"A what now?"

"A mortal born with the ability to heal magical beings and realms." Jack breaks free of the ice at his feet. "They're incredibly rare. The last one..."

"Was your mother." Gabriel hurls another icy attack, but this time, Jack deflects it easily. "And look how well that turned out for her."

The air crackles with power as Jack steps forward, his hand finding mine. Energy surges between us—not just his winter magic or my apparent healing ability, but something new. Something balanced.

"You're wrong, Gabriel." Ice spreads from Jack's feet, but instead of the usual stark white, it shimmers with rainbow hues where it touches my shoes. "I watched her over the years. She made her choice and chose love."

Gabriel's face contorts with rage. "No. I won't let you ruin everything I've worked for."

He launches an attack against us, but the moment his ice magic connects with our joined hands, it transforms. The frozen spears turn to delicate frost flowers, their edges glowing with that same opalescent light I'd seen in the courtyard.

*We're not destroying his power*, I realize. *We're transforming it.*

I stumble back as Gabriel launches another attack, forcing Jack and me to break apart. Our joined hands slip away from each other as we dodge in opposite directions. Losing contact leaves me cold and hollow inside.

"You can't dance forever!" Gabriel snarls, hurling a barrage of ice daggers at me.

I throw up my hands instinctively. A burst of golden light erupts from my palms, melting his projectiles into harmless droplets. Across the room, Jack deflects Gabriel's frost with precise movements, his own ice magic crackling through the air.

"Jack!" I call out, watching him weave and pivot. His eyes meet mine and understanding passes between us. We start moving toward each other, dodging and countering Gabriel's increasingly desperate attacks.

The moment our fingers touch again, that incredible sensation returns—like a perfect winter morning, crisp yet somehow warm.

Each blast Gabriel sends our way transforms into something beautiful rather than destructive. Ice daggers become delicate snowflakes. Deadly frost turns to intricate crystal patterns in the air.

"You only saw what you wanted to see." Jack's voice rumbles through me where our hands connect. "Just like you twisted everything else to serve your purposes."

I squeeze Jack's hand. *He needs to know.* "The prophecy wasn't about destruction. It was about change—necessary change."

"The old ways crumbling..." Jack's eyes widen with understanding.

"Because they needed to." The words flow through me with absolute certainty. "Winter isn't meant to be isolated. It's part of a cycle."

Gabriel backs away, his face contorting. "No. I won't let centuries of work be undone by some mortal."

He raises both hands, and the temperature plummets. Ice crawls up the walls, darker and sharper than anything I've seen in this realm. Jack steps closer to me, our joined magic creating a protective sphere around us.

"Your healing nature." Jack's voice is soft despite the chaos. "That's what I felt from the beginning. What I fought against because I thought it would weaken my power."

"When really, it completes it."

The truth of it sings through our connected magic. This is what was always meant to be—not destruction, but balance. Not weakness, but strength shared.

Gabriel snarls and hurls himself forward, as ice shards attack us from all sides. A blade of black ice is forming in his hand like a jagged dagger pulled from the depths of winter itself. Our combined magic meets his attack, but he pushes through, aiming straight for my heart.

"Violet!" Jack's voice cracks with desperation as he shoves me aside, his hands rough against my ribs.

The ice blade catches him in the shoulder instead of my chest, the sickening sound of it tearing through flesh and muscle making my stomach lurch. Dark blood wells up, staining his white shirt crimson. He stumbles backward, and our magical connection snaps like a thread pulled too tight.

Gabriel's triumphant laugh echoes off the ice walls as Jack falls to one knee, his face twisted in pain.

*Fuck. This is my fault. All my fucking fault.*

"Still so predictable, brother. Always trying to protect others." Gabriel twists the blade, and Jack groans. "Now watch as I finish what I started."

He turns toward me, another blade forming, but I don't back away. The power still hums under my skin, different without Jack's touch but no less real. I am a healer, not just of bodies, but of magic itself.

I lunge toward Jack, my fingers stretching desperately to reach him.

The moment my fingers brush Jack's arm, power surges between us. His eyes meet mine, and understanding flows without words. The connection feels different now—not just winter's chill, but something deeper, like roots stretching through frozen soil seeking life.

*Trust me*, I think, and somehow I know he hears it.

Jack's hand closes over mine. The black ice in his shoulder begins to glow where my fingers touch it, transforming from Gabriel's corrupt magic into something pure.

"Impossible." Gabriel's blade wavers. "You can't—"

"Can't what?" My free hand reaches toward him. "Can't heal what you've broken? Can't restore what you've twisted?"

The power flowing through me feels ancient and new all at once. Every injury I've ever treated, every life I've helped save, it wasn't just medical training. It was preparation for this.

"Stay back." Gabriel retreats a step, his confident mask cracking. "You don't understand what you're dealing with."

"I understand perfectly." The words rise from somewhere deep inside, where knowledge I didn't know I had awakens. "You're out of balance. Just like this realm. Just like the prophecy tried to warn about."

Jack rises beside me, his shoulder healed where my touch transformed Gabriel's ice. Our joined magic creates a sphere of swirling frost and light around us. Where the energies meet, they don't fight—they dance.

"The prophecy spoke of falls and loss." Gabriel's voice shakes. "Of destruction..."

"No." The certainty rings through me. "It spoke of change. Of trust. Of healing what centuries of isolation damaged."

My magic—my true healing nature—reaches for Gabriel. Not to harm, but to help. To restore what's been corrupted by anger and jealousy.

Gabriel backs away, his gray eyes wide with something that looks almost like fear. "Don't."

"Let me help you." I take a step forward, Jack's strength flowing through our connection. "This isn't what you really want."

For just a moment, I see something flicker in Gabriel's expression—a glimpse of ancient pain, of loneliness that mirrors what I sensed in Jack. Then his face hardens.

"You know nothing of what I want."

He raises his hands, darkness gathering around them like storm clouds. The temperature plunges so low it burns.

The temperature drop makes my bones ache, but Jack's warmth through our connection keeps me steady. Gabriel's magic coalesces into a massive wave of darkness, like a tsunami made of shadow and ice.

*This is it. His final play.*

"You could have been part of this." My voice carries despite the howling wind. "Could have helped us make it better."

Gabriel's response is a roar that shakes the crystalline walls. The wave of darkness crashes toward us, and for a moment, I can't breathe through the sheer weight of his hatred.

Jack's hand tightens on mine. Our magic surges, stronger together than apart. Where Gabriel's power is jagged and cold, ours flows like a river in spring—powerful but life-giving.

*Let me help*, I push the thought through our connection. Jack's energy meshes with mine, winter's chill softened by healing warmth.

The wave hits our combined shield. His ice crystals form and shatter around us, but they can't penetrate the swirling barrier of our joined magic. Gabriel's attack splinters against it like waves on rocks.

"Now, Jack."

He understands without further explanation. Our power flows outward, meeting Gabriel's darkness, not with destruction but with transformation. Where our magic touches his, the corrupt ice begins to change—becoming clear, pure.

"No!" Gabriel tries to pull back, but it's too late.

The transformation races up his arms, turning his dark ice to crystal. He struggles, but each movement only speeds the process. Within seconds, he's encased in a pristine prison of his own magic, purified by our combined power.

"Is he..." I step closer, studying Gabriel's frozen form. His eyes are open, aware.

"Contained." Jack's voice rumbles with both relief and sadness. "The crystal will hold him until we decide what to do."

I press my hand to the surface of Gabriel's prison. Even through the crystal, I can sense the turmoil in his magic, the centuries of pain and bitterness that twisted it into something dark.

"We can help him, eventually. When he's ready."

Jack's arm slides around my waist, pulling me close. "You truly are a healer."

"Yeah, well." I lean into his embrace, exhausted but satisfied. "Someone has to keep you frosty boys in line."

I glance around the throne room, taking in the aftermath of our battle. Jagged ice fragments cover the ground, catching the light like fallen stars. My body aches, but the warmth of Jack's embrace soothes the worst of it.

Something green catches my eye above us—a sprig of mistletoe hanging from an ice archway. *How did I never notice that before?*

"Is that mistletoe in a winter palace?"

Jack follows my gaze, his lips curving into a rare smile.

"An ancient tradition. The Norse believed mistletoe was sacred to Frigg, goddess of love. When her son Baldr was killed by a mistletoe arrow, her tears turned the berries white. She decreed it would forever be a symbol of love, not death."

"That... surprisingly sweet for a winter legend."

"There's more." His fingers trace along my jaw. "Winter spirits once used mistletoe to bind promises. A kiss beneath it seals intentions more surely than any oath."

Heat floods my cheeks. "Are you saying mistletoe is like magical mistletoe?"

"All mistletoe has power. But here, in this realm..." His voice drops lower, making my body tremble. "Here it's a bridge between warmth and cold, life and sleep, mortal and immortal."

"So what happens if we..." I gesture vaguely upward.

Jack's laugh rumbles through his chest. "Would you like to find out?"

Before I can answer, he cups my face in his hands. His touch is cool but not cold.

When his lips meet mine, magic sparks between us—not the raw power we wielded against Gabriel, but something softer, deeper. The mistletoe above us begins to glow with a gentle silver light.

*This is what the prophecy means*, I realize as Jack deepens the kiss. Not the end of winter, but the beginning of something new.

Jack pulls back just enough to rest his forehead against mine. "I can feel you," he whispers. "Not just physically. I can feel your essence, your warmth."

"Is that the mistletoe's magic?"

"No." His thumb traces my lower lip. "That's all us. The mistletoe just... amplifies what's already there."

## Chapter Twenty-One

# JACK

The weight of my crown feels different now as I hold it in my hands, studying the ice crystals that have sustained my realm for centuries. My chambers feel hollow without Violet's warmth, though she rests just down the hall, recovering from Gabriel's attack.

*I almost lost her. My stubbornness nearly cost everything.*

Rising from my desk, I gather my magic and craft a second crown from the eternal ice—this one a delicate circlet meant for Violet. Frost flowers bloom along its gentle curves, and each crystal captures light like the opalescent glow I first saw when Violet touched my sculptures.

With a final wave of my hand, I add matching frost flowers to my crown as well, letting them wind between the deadly points. A reminder that even the harshest winter can harbor beauty.

My feet carry me to her door before I can second-guess myself. The guard steps aside with a respectful nod.

I pause, my knuckles hovering over the wood. "Violet?"

"Come in." Her voice sounds tired but steady.

She's propped up against pillows, her brown hair tousled, dark circles under her eyes from exhausting her magic. The sight of her drained and vulnerable makes my chest ache.

"I have something for you."

"If it's another lecture about staying in bed, save it. The nurse in me knows better than you do."

A small smile tugs at my lips. Even injured, her fire burns bright. I move to sit on the edge of her bed; the circlet cradled in my palms.

"This is an apology. And a promise. I was wrong. About everything. The prophecy, your presence here, what I thought would destroy my kingdom."

I trace one of the frost flowers with my finger. "You were never meant to be my downfall. You are my salvation."

"Pretty words don't fix everything."

"No. But actions might." I hold out the circlet. "This is crafted from my own power, bound with ancient winter magic. By giving it to you, I'm sharing my strength, my kingdom... my heart. If you'll have them."

Her fingers brush mine as she touches the crown, and that familiar opalescent glow spreads through the ice. "You risked everything to save me from Gabriel."

"I would do it again. A thousand times over."

A tear slides down her cheek, but she's smiling. "Help me put it on?"

With gentle hands, I place the circlet on her head. The frost flowers seem to come alive, tiny crystals dancing in her hair. She's never looked more beautiful.

"I promise you, Violet Jones, I will spend every day proving worthy of being your mate."

Her breath catches as I lean forward, drawn by the way the crystals reflect in her eyes. The scent of her—warm vanilla and something uniquely Violet—fills my senses. My fingertips trace the edge of the circlet where it meets her temple.

"It suits you." My voice comes out rougher than intended.

"Does this mean I get to boss people around now, too?" A playful smile tugs at her lips.

*Even after everything, she can still make me want to smile.*

"You've been 'bossing people around' since the moment you arrived." I brush a strand of hair behind her ear. "The crown merely makes it official."

She catches my hand before I can withdraw it, her warm fingers wrapping around my cool ones. "Speaking of official... we need to talk about what happened with Gabriel."

The name sends ice crackling along my fingertips. "He will never harm you again."

"That's not what I meant." She shifts closer, wincing slightly at the movement. "Jack, he is your brother. All those centuries of manipulation... are you okay?"

*Am I okay?* The question catches me off guard. No one has asked me that in... I can't remember how long.

"I should be asking you that. You pushed yourself too hard with magic today. Your body isn't used to channeling that much power."

"Stop deflecting." Her grip tightens on my hand. "I saw your face when he revealed the truth."

The memory of Gabriel's betrayal burns like frost-bite. "I trusted him. For centuries, I let him guide my decisions, shape my beliefs." My free hand clenches into a fist. "I let him convince me to push you away."

"Hey." She places her other hand over my fist until it relaxes. "You figured it out. You chose to listen when I brought you the truth, even though it meant questioning everything you believed." She grins. "Eventually."

"Too late. You could have died."

"But I didn't." She tugs my hand until I meet her gaze. "And now we're stronger. Together."

The word settles something in my chest that's been restless since Gabriel's attack. *Together.* No more isolation, no more walls of ice between us.

The tenderness in Violet's eyes makes my chest ache. I don't deserve her forgiveness, not after everything I put her through.

Yet here she sits, still holding my hand like I'm something precious rather than the fool who nearly destroyed us both.

"You were protecting your kingdom." She traces the frost patterns on my skin. "I understand that now."

I shake my head. "Don't make excuses for my behavior. I was a coward."

"Maybe." A small smile plays at her lips. "But you're *my* coward."

Her possessive words stir something deep inside me, a warmth previously unfamiliar to my frozen heart. She tries to adjust her position, exhaustion clear in her movements after expending so much magical energy. Her powers have left her drained, yet that teasing smile remains.

"Here, let me—"

"No." She holds up a hand, stopping my attempt to help. "I need to do this properly."

Violet takes a deep breath, then slides from the bed to kneel before me. The crown I gave her catches the light, sending rainbow prisms dancing across her face. My throat tightens at the sight.

"Jack Frost, I pledge myself to you and this realm." Her voice rings with conviction. "Not because of prophecy or fate, but because I choose to. Because I've seen your heart beneath all that ice, and it's more beautiful than any sculpture in your garden."

*This impossible woman.* Even wronged, she finds ways to humble me.

"I believe in you." She presses her palm against my chest, right over my thundering heart. "In us. And I swear, by whatever power brought me here, I will never let anyone make you doubt yourself again."

Magic surges between us at her words, pure and powerful. Ice crystals form in the air, catching light like stars, and beneath her touch, my skin glows with that same opalescent light from the first time she touched my sculptures.

"Violet..." My voice breaks on her name.

She rises up from her knees, bringing her face level with mine.

"I'm not finished. Your brother was wrong about everything. You're not weak for feeling. You're strongest when you let yourself feel everything."

The truth of her words resonates through my entire being. I cup her face in my hands, marveling at how she leans into my icy touch without hesitation.

"How did I ever think you would destroy my kingdom?" The words come out rough with emotion. "You've already made it more magnificent than I ever could alone."

Her hands slide up my chest, fingers tracing the frost patterns racing across my skin. "I love you, Jack. Not the Winter King, not Jack Frost. Just you."

My heart stops. Her words echo in my mind as I study every detail of her face, searching for any hint of deception. The raw honesty in her expression steals my breath. My voice comes out rough with need.

"Say it again."

She smiles up at me, reaching up to brush a stray lock of hair from my eyes.

"I love you, Jack Frost. I love the winter in your heart and the warmth you bring to mine."

My heart pounds against my ribs. Centuries of isolation crack and fall away like ice in spring.

"I love you too, Violet. You've melted every wall I built. Made me feel things I thought died long ago." I press my forehead to hers, breathing in her warmth. "You are my heart, my home, my everything."

"Then stop fighting this—fighting us." Her lips brush against mine as she speaks. "Let yourself have this happiness. Let yourself have me."

I pull her closer, my magic wrapping around us both in swirls of frost and starlight.

"I'm done fighting. You're mine, and I'm yours. Forever."

Her eyes shine with unshed tears, but her smile could melt glaciers. "That's what happens when you let love in, my mate."

## Chapter Twenty-Two
# VIOLET

The bright winter moonlight filters through the icy dome above, casting rainbow and shadows across the gathered crowd. My heart thunders against my ribs as I fidget with the delicate silver chains adorning my white gown. The dress itself seems spun from freshly fallen snow, intricate frost patterns woven throughout the fabric.

*How did I end up here? A month ago, I was just a nurse in Colorado.*

The great hall stretches before me, filled with winter fae in their finest attire. Their ethereal beauty makes me feel small and plain. Yet the warmth in their eyes as they bow tells me I've been accepted as their future lady.

Winter sprites dance through the air, their crystalline wings catching the light like prisms. Massive yeti lumber by in surprisingly elegant robes of white and silver. Ice nymphs glide across the floor, their skin sparkling like fresh snow. Even the goblin delegation, despite their warty appearances, wear suits of frost-covered velvet that put my elegant dress to shame.

I spot what must be a snow phoenix perched in the rafters, its white and blue flames casting shifting shadows across the gathered crowd. Each creature radiates magic and power in a way that reminds me just how much I didn't feel like I belonged in this world of immortal winter beings.

"Stop fussing." Cora adjusts my crown of white roses and crystal snowflakes. "You look perfect."

"I'm not fussing." I drop my hands to my sides. "I'm having a fucking existential crisis."

She grins. "Save that for after the ceremony." She smooths down my skirts. "Jack's waiting."

My breath catches at the mention of his name. Through our strengthened bond, I feel his anticipation mixing with my own. At the far end of the great hall, beneath another arch woven with mistletoe and ice flowers, Jack stands tall in his formal attire. His white hair is pulled back beneath his crown of crystal spires, and his ice-blue eyes find mine across the distance.

*My mate. My equal. My match in every way.*

The music starts—an otherworldly melody that makes my skin tingle. As I take my first step forward, frost spirals out from beneath my feet, creating delicate patterns across the marble floor. My newfound powers still surprise me, but they feel right, like they've always been a part of me waiting to emerge.

Jack's face softens as I approach, a smile playing at his lips. Gone is the cold, distant ruler who first brought me here. In his place stands the man who risked everything to protect me, who learned to trust in our bond despite centuries of fear.

"Little mate," he murmurs as I reach him, his deep voice carrying in the hushed hall.

"Your Frostiness." I smirk at his eye roll. Some things never change.

Above us, the mistletoe seems to pulse with an inner light. Jack takes my hands in his. "The ancients believed mistletoe held the power to bridge worlds."

I squeeze his hands. "Like us?"

"Like us." His thumb traces the silver mark on my wrist—the visible sign of our bond. "A bridge between realms, between power and healing, between what was and what could be."

Jack's magic thrums through the hall as he begins the ancient binding words. The temperature drops, and ice crystals form in the air around us, suspended like stars.

A familiar laugh breaks through the ethereal atmosphere.

"Only you would manage to find a husband who makes it snow indoors during the ceremony." Alana's voice carries from the front row.

Heat floods my cheeks. When Jack insisted on bringing her here for the ceremony, I'd warned him about her complete inability to maintain proper decorum. *At least she's wearing the formal gown Cora picked out instead of her scrubs.*

"I assure you, the weather manifestations are entirely intentional." Jack's formal tone has that slight edge that means he's trying not to smile.

"Oh my god, you actually made him defensive." I turn to Alana. "I didn't think that was possible."

"I'm not defensive." Frost creeps along the floor around his feet.

"Your ice says otherwise, big guy."

The winter fae gathered around us titter with barely contained laughter. Jack's shoulders relax slightly at the sound. It's exactly what this ceremony needed—a reminder that love shouldn't be all solemnity and protocol.

"If we could continue?" Jack raises an eyebrow at me, but I catch the amusement in his eyes.

"By all means. Proceed with your weather magic."

He lifts our joined hands, and pure power courses between us. My healing magic rises to meet his winter essence, creating swirls of golden light that dance with his ice crystals. The sight draws gasps from the crowd.

A ray of winter sun pierces through the sky, the light catching each ice crystal, sending sparkles dancing across the faces of everyone watching. I can't look away from how beautiful it is—like the northern lights condensed into our joined hands.

"As winter and summer find balance," Jack's voice resonates through the hall, "so too shall our realms exist in harmony."

The magic builds, lifting my hair in an ethereal breeze. Through our bond, I feel Jack's wonder at how perfectly our powers complement each other. No longer fighting against nature, but working with it.

"Holy shit," Alana whispers loudly enough for everyone to hear. "That's actually real magic."

"Told you I wasn't hallucinating." I wink at her, earning another round of chuckles from the crowd.

Jack squeezes my hands, drawing my attention back to him. "Are you quite finished disrupting our sacred ceremony?"

"Not even close." I grin up at him. "You knew what you were getting into when you decided to keep me."

His expression softens into that rare, genuine smile that still makes my heart skip. "Indeed, I did, little mate. Indeed, I did."

---

I adjust my crown for the hundredth time, still not used to its weight, as another well-wisher approaches. Jack's hand rests at the small of my back, his thumb making small circles that send pleasant tingles up my spine.

"I still can't believe you married the actual Jack Frost." Alana shakes her head, champagne glass in hand. "Like, the one who makes snow days happen."

"Among other things." I lean into Jack's solid frame.

"And you're sure about this whole ice princess thing?"

"Lady," Jack corrects, his voice carrying that formal tone he uses with others. "She's my Lady."

I bite back a smile at his possessiveness. "I'm sure, Alana. More sure than I've ever been about anything."

Jack shifts beside me, his fingers pressing more firmly against my back. When I glance up, I catch him staring at my lips.

"Well, you two are sickeningly cute together." Alana downs the rest of her champagne. "Though I still say this place needs better heating."

"The cold doesn't bother me anymore." I reach up to touch the delicate frost flowers adorning my crown. "Side effect of being Winter's mate."

Jack's breath hitches. His ice-blue eyes darken as they meet mine, and the temperature around us drops several degrees.

"Okay, that's my cue to mingle elsewhere." Alana backs away with a knowing smirk. "Don't freeze anyone while I'm gone."

I barely register her departure. Jack's hand slides to my hip, pulling me closer. "We should leave," he murmurs against my ear.

"We have guests—"

"They can celebrate without us." His lips brush my temple, leaving a trail of frost that melts instantly against my warm skin. "I've waited centuries for you. I don't want to wait another moment."

The raw need in his voice makes my heart race. "Jack..."

"Please."

That single word, spoken so softly, breaks my resolve. I nod, and a rare smile spreads across his face.

My heart pounds in my chest as Jack's transporting magic swirls around us, a dizzying rush of frost and wind that whisks us away from the celebration.

The world blurs, a kaleidoscope of icy blues and stark whites, and then we're standing in the heart of our private chambers. The air here is thick with the scent of pine and the faint, sweet perfume of frost flowers.

Jack's hands are on me before my feet have fully adjusted to the solid ground, his touch both gentle and insatiable.

"I need you," he breathes, the words a whispered vow against my lips.

I answer with a soft moan, my body already aching for his. My fingers find the clasp of his ceremonial cloak, tugging it free so that the heavy fabric pools at his feet. Beneath, his suit is a sleek, dark contrast to his pale blue skin, and I trace the line of his broad shoulders, the muscles taut with anticipation.

He catches my wrists, pulling me closer, and the room temperature plummets. Tiny crystals of ice dance in the air, swirling around us like a private snowstorm.

"You are my undoing," he murmurs, his voice a low rumble that I feel in my bones.

His mouth crashes into mine with fierce hunger, his tongue claiming every inch as his hands grip my hips and pull me hard against him.

"You are my thaw," his frost-touched lips brush my ear. His words send heat pooling between my legs.

I raise onto my tiptoes, pressing my lips to the column of his throat. His skin is cool against my mouth, his body trembles as my lips trace a path to his ear.

"Then melt for me," I murmur, pressing my body against his, my fingers tracing patterns on his chest.

With a swift motion, Jack lifts me off my feet, carrying me to the massive bed draped in furs and velvet.

He lays me down with a reverence that makes my chest tighten, his gaze never leaving mine as he begins to remove his suit. Each piece of clothing he discards reveals more of the sculpted physique that's as much a part of winter as the snowflakes that fall outside our window.

I reach out as he stands before me wearing only his trousers, but he shakes his head, a wicked smile playing on his lips.

"Let me," he says, his hands deftly working at the fastenings of my gown. The fabric parts under his touch, baring my skin to the chill air. I gasp as the cold meets my heated flesh, goosebumps rising in its wake.

Jack leans down, his mouth following the trail of his fingers, each kiss leaving behind a tingling sensation that's both cool and fiery.

His hands slide up my thighs, pushing the fabric of my gown aside, and I'm helpless to do anything but let him. The cool air is replaced by the warmth of his breath, and I can't suppress the moan that escapes my lips as his tongue finds me.

My body trembles under his touch, caught between the burning warmth of his tongue and the frost-laden magic flowing from his lips.

He knows exactly how to use his powers, switching between scalding heat and arctic chill until I'm writhing beneath him. My fingers tangle in his silver hair as waves of pleasure crash through me, each stroke of his tongue sending sparks of electricity racing along my nerves.

When he hums against my flesh, the vibration combined with his alternating temperatures makes my thighs quiver and my back arch off the bed.

I'm panting now, my fingers tangled in his frosted white hair, holding him to me as the first waves of my orgasm build. Jack's magic pulses around us, the air crackling with energy as he brings me closer and closer to the edge.

And then, with a final, dizzying flick of his tongue, I'm falling, my body convulsing with the force of my release. The room around us brightens with a soft, ethereal glow, our combined magic reacting to the intensity of our connection.

As I ride out the aftershocks, Jack moves over me, his eyes dark with desire.

"You are my everything." His words pulse through our bond, and I can feel that he means it, with every fiber of his being.

I pull him down to me, our lips meeting in a kiss that's both a promise and a plea. I need him inside me, need to feel that completeness that only would come when we're joined together.

"Make love to me, Jack," I murmur against his mouth. "Show me the depth of winter's heart."

Jack's eyes darken to a deep cobalt and his expression softens, a warmth spreading through his usually icy demeanor that ignites something deep inside me. He keeps his hands on my body as we stand from the bed, guiding me toward the window seat where moonlight spills across plush cushions.

"You're sure?" he whispers against my lips, his breath hot and trembling with raw desire.

"I've never been more certain of anything," I tell him, my fingers threading through his hair as I pull him down into a kiss that burns with urgency.

My arms lock around his neck, and I rise onto my toes, pressing my body flush against his. His mouth tastes like the heart of winter—sharp and pure, like crystalline air just before a snowfall. Each breath he takes seems to steal oxygen from my lungs, leaving me dizzy and desperate, wanting nothing more than to be consumed by him completely.

"Violet," he groans as I nip at his bottom lip. His hands slide down to grip my hips, lifting me onto the cushioned seat. I part my thighs so he can step between them, our bodies fitting together perfectly.

"Touch me," I beg, arching into him as his hands roam over my skin with reverent possession. His mouth blazes a path of kisses down my throat, each press of his lips sending sparks of pleasure coursing through me.

"Please, Jack. I need you."

"You have me," he vows between kisses. "All of me."

His fingers dig into my hips as I grind against him, needing to feel every inch of his body against mine. My breasts press into his chest, nipples hardening at the friction. I moan into his mouth as his tongue explores mine, tasting and teasing.

"Fuck, you feel so good," I gasp as his mouth trails down my neck, teeth grazing my sensitive skin.

"You're so beautiful," he murmurs, his warm breath ghosting over my skin.

I run my fingers through his hair, gripping tight as his mouth continues to explore my body.

"I love you," I whisper.

He closes his eyes at my words, a shudder running through him. "You make me feel," he says, his voice rough, "Things I swore I'd never feel again."

I stroke his cheek, gently urging him to look at me. "Let me show you what it's like to love and be loved in return."

His eyes open, a swirl of emotions in their icy depths. He searches my face as if he's afraid to hope, and then, slowly, a smile breaks across his face. It's a smile that transforms him, softening his features and making him look younger, almost vulnerable.

"Show me," he says, his voice soft.

And I do.

I leave my perch on the window seat and press against him. My hands find his shoulders as I rise on my tiptoes, pressing my lips against his.

The kiss starts gentle, exploring, but quickly turns hungry and desperate. His mouth opens under mine, and I slip my tongue inside, tasting him. He groans, the sound vibrating through me. His hands slide into my hair, holding me close as our tongues dance and tangle. Heat builds between us with each passing second, turning my blood to liquid fire.

I press closer, wanting—needing—more of him.

I break the kiss, trailing my lips down his jaw, nipping at his earlobe before I continue my descent.

His breath hitches as I reach the waistband of his pants and my hands work at his belt, pulling it free before I tackle the button and zipper of his pants. I can feel his erection straining against the fabric, and I'm eager to set it free.

I pull his pants and boxers down just enough to release his cock, thick and hard and ready for me.

My mouth waters at the sight of him, his impressive length decorated with intricate swirls of frost that spiral up the thick shaft. His cock stands proud, the pale blue-white patterns making it look almost ethereal against his blue skin.

*Holy fuck, he's perfect.* He's thick—thicker than I expected, and even his balls are dusted with a light coating of frost, like they've been touched by winter itself. The delicate crystalline designs seem to pulse with his heartbeat, and I can't wait to trace them with my tongue.

"Beautiful," I whisper, stroking the velvet-soft skin. His breath hitches as my thumb traces one of the glowing spirals. Pre-cum beads at his slit, clear and glistening like melting ice, and his cock twitches under my hungry gaze.

I remember his words from earlier, how he'd teased me about my filthy mouth. Now, I'm about to show him just how dirty I can be.

I push him back on the window seat and meet his gaze again, holding it as I sink to my knees before him. His eyes widen, a mix of surprise and anticipation flashing across his face.

"You're so fucking gorgeous," I breathe, wrapping my hand around the base of his cock, stroking him slowly as I lean forward and flick my tongue over the tip. "And you taste even better."

He sucks in a sharp breath, his body tensing under my touch. Encouraged by his reaction, I take him into my mouth, my lips sealing around his shaft as I start to move.

I bob my head, taking him deeper with each stroke, my tongue swirling around his length. His hands tangle in my hair, not guiding but simply holding on as I work him over. I can feel him getting closer, his thighs trembling beneath my arm, his breaths coming faster and faster.

"Fuck, Violet," he groans, his voice strained. "Just like that. Don't stop."

I have no intention of stopping. I increase my pace, sucking him harder, deeper, until he's gasping my name, his body arching off the cushion as he comes undone.

He tastes like fresh mint and frozen berries, a sweet winter chill that makes my mouth tingle. I swallow every drop, not letting up until he's spent and trembling beneath my hands.

I sit back on my heels, a smug smile playing on my lips as I watch him come down from his high.

"You know, you taste better than any dessert I've had in ages," I say with a smirk, running my tongue over my lips.

His eyes are dark with desire, and there's a raw, unguarded quality to his expression that I've never seen before.

"My turn," he growls, pulling me up and onto his lap. His mouth finds my breast, his tongue teasing my nipple into a tight peak as his fingers toy with the other.

His mouth trails down my neck, nibbling and sucking at the sensitive skin. I arch my back, offering myself to him as his hands skim down my body, leaving goose bumps in their wake.

"Jack," I breathe, my voice a pleading whisper.

He chuckles, the vibrations tickling my skin. "Patience," his voice is a husky whisper. "I plan to enjoy this."

His hands find my hips, guiding me as I move against him. Our breath comes in sharp gasps, our magic crackling around us like a symphony of winter and desire.

His hands glide up my sides, his touch feather-light, making me ache for more. His fingers trail over my collarbones, down the curve of my shoulder, and then lower, until he's cupping my breasts. I moan at the contact, my head falling back as he teases my peaks to tight buds.

"You're so responsive," he murmurs, his lips finding the sensitive skin of my neck. "So perfect."

His eyes lock with mine, a storm of desire and tenderness swirling in their icy depths. I reach up to trace the sharp line of his jaw, marveling at how his skin feels both cool and burning beneath my touch.

My hands slide down his chest, feeling the rapid beat of his heart beneath my palms.

How did I ever think him cold?

"My mate," he whispers against my throat, his breath making me arch up against him. "My queen."

I thread my fingers through his hair, holding him to me as my hips continue their slow, sensuous dance.

"I want you," I breathe, my voice laced with need.

"I'm yours," he says, his voice a low growl. "Always."

I grind against him, feeling his still rock-hard cock pressing against my clit. I'm already wet, already aching for him, and I can't wait any longer. I reach between us, positioning him at my entrance before I sink down onto him.

We both moan as he fills me completely, his massive cock stretching me in the most delicious way. The unique texture of his shaft sends jolts of pleasure through my core. It's smooth and cool, like polished ice, with raised frost patterns that swirl and pulse against my walls. I wrap my legs around his hips, drawing him closer, gasping at how deep he reaches.

I start to move, riding him with slow, deliberate strokes that quickly build into a frenzied pace. The temperature of his cock fluctuates with his passion—cooling then heating, driving me wild with the contrasting sensations.

He meets me thrust for thrust, his hands gripping my hips tightly as we chase our climax together. His size and power overwhelm my senses—he's larger than any mortal man, filling me completely.

Each powerful snap of his hips sends a new wave of magic through the room, ice crystals dancing in the air like stars. The frost patterns on his body glow brilliantly now, matching the intensity building between us.

I pant, grinding down harder onto his thick length. The cool ridges of frost stimulate spots inside me I didn't know existed.

"Jack," I breathe, my head falling back as he sets a steady rhythm. "Fuck, you feel amazing." Every movement feels like perfection, like pieces of a puzzle finally clicking into place.

The world around us fades away, leaving only the two of us and the raw, intense connection that's threatening to consume us both. I can feel the tension coiling low in my belly, each stroke bringing me closer and closer to the edge.

"Come for me, Violet," he whispers, his voice rough with need. "Let go. I've got you."

With his words echoing in my ears, I do. I shatter around him, my body convulsing with the force of my orgasm. He follows me over the edge, his own release triggering a second wave of pleasure that leaves me boneless and sated in his arms.

A tingling sensation spreads across my skin where Jack touches me. Delicate patterns of frost bloom and spiral outward, like ice crystals forming on a winter window. The intricate designs glitter in the light, spreading up my arm and across my chest.

My breath catches as I watch golden lines emerge on Jack's pale blue skin in response—they pulse and glow like molten metal, tracing ancient symbols I don't understand.

The magic pulses between us, hot and cold, light and dark, until I can't tell where my essence ends and his begins.

We are one now, sealed by forces beyond mortal understanding. The bond settles into my bones, into my very being, permanent and unbreakable.

"Fuck," I whisper, tracing a finger along one of the shimmering patterns. The magic sparks at my touch, sending waves of pleasure through my oversensitive body.

Jack's eyes darken as he watches the designs complete themselves across our skin. "Now you understand. There's no going back."

His forehead presses against mine, our breaths mingling in the space between us. I can feel his power pulsing through my veins, mixing with my own in ways that make the very air around us sing.

The frost flowers on the side table burst into bloom, their petals dancing in rhythm with our bodies, and the walls come alive with intricate designs, glowing like the fire burning within me.

*So, the prophecy was right.* I think through the haze of pleasure. *Not destruction, but creation—a balance.* I grin, feeling the power of our connection.

*And damn, is it hot.*

## Chapter Twenty-Three

# JACK

The dungeons beneath my castle hold memories I'd rather forget.

Each step down the frost-covered stairs echoes with the weight of centuries of isolation and betrayal. The magical barriers shimmer with an opalescent glow, containing my brother's considerable power.

Gabriel sits cross-legged on the floor, his back against the stone wall. The formal attire he always wears is wrinkled and stained. His usual smirk is gone, replaced by something darker.

"Come to gloat, *brother*?" The last word drips with venom.

My fingers curl into fists. "I want answers."

"About what? How I deceived you? How I hid things from you?" He stands, moving closer to the barrier. "Or perhaps about our dear father?"

The temperature plummets several degrees, frost creeping across the stone floor between us. "All of it."

"Did you know our father had a taste for fae women?" Gabriel's gray eyes flash with a dangerous light. "My mother was a noble in his court. When she became pregnant, he cast her out of his kingdom and into the mortal realm to die like a dog in the streets."

*Like father, like son.* The thought makes bile rise in my throat, acid burning the back of my tongue. How many fucking times had I pushed Violet away, terrified she would destroy everything I'd built? That she would shatter the careful control I'd maintained for centuries?

"She survived long enough to birth me and raise me for a while, but being away from the magical realm killed her slowly, painfully."

I watch Gabriel stalk back and forth in his prison. His steps remind me of a wild animal—dangerous and ready to strike at any moment.

"I grew up alone in the mortal world." He frowns. "Learning to control powers I didn't understand. When I finally found my way back to this realm, I arrived at court with my most charming smile and polished manners."

His hands clench at the memory, frost crackling across his knuckles. "Father took me in, gave me his time and wisdom without knowing who I truly was."

I remember the day Gabriel first appeared at court, charming and polite, playing the role of an eager noble seeking patronage. No one suspected his true identity then. He ingratiated himself with the courtiers, learned our customs, and caught our father's eye with his quick wit and natural affinity for winter magic.

"The lies tasted bitter on my tongue each time I bowed, each time I played the role of an ambitious noble seeking his favor." He paces the length of the room, his footsteps leaving patches of ice in their wake and the temperature drops several degrees. "But I needed to know him, to understand the man who had abandoned my mother."

A bitter laugh escapes him. "Then it happened—his eyes went wide as he finally saw it. My mother's fae features staring back at him from my face. The woman he'd fucked and thrown away like garbage."

His fingers curl into fists. "The truth poured out between us, toxic and raw. He kept me at court, sure. Gave me a fancy title and tasks to occupy my time."

The temperature plummets as rage burns cold in his eyes. "But his words fucking gutted me worse than any knife could: 'Jack remains my only true heir.' Because that's all I'd ever be to him—the bastard son who could never measure up to his precious legitimate prince."

*Perhaps that's when the seeds of hatred took root.* I watch my half-brother pace, remembering how Father grew increasingly unstable in those final years, jumping at shadows and muttering about prophecies.

His paranoia poisoned everything, including whatever fragile bond might have formed between Gabriel and me. Now I wonder if Father saw something coming that the rest of us missed.

"You could have told me the truth from the beginning," I say, my voice hard as ice. "We might have been brothers in more than just blood."

"And risk you rejecting me like our father rejected my mother?" He laughs, the sound brittle as breaking ice. "No, I needed to earn my place first. To prove I was worthy of the throne he wanted to deny me by birthright."

The words hit me like shards of ice straight to the chest. How many times had I done the same to Violet? Pushed her away because I deemed her unworthy of my position, my power, my cursed bloodline?

"Your mate showed me an uncomfortable truth," Gabriel says, his mouth twisting in disgust. "That wallowing in misery and revenge isn't the only fucking option. Though I still want to watch this entire realm burn."

*Violet*. My chest constricts with the memory of her forgiveness, her stubborn willingness to see past my coldness and fear, to reach the man buried beneath centuries of ice.

"She forgave me," I say quietly, the words barely more than a whisper. "Even after everything I did to push her away."

"How fortunate for you." Gabriel's voice drips with bitterness like poison. "Some of us weren't blessed with such understanding souls in our lives."

"You could be." The words surprise even me as they leave my mouth. "If you're willing to let go of the past that haunts you."

Gabriel stares at me, searching my face with an intensity that burns. "You sound like her now. All that talk of redemption and second chances."

"Because she showed me there's strength in forgiveness, not weakness." I place my hand against the magical barrier separating us, feeling its energy hum against my palm. "You're my brother, Gabriel. Despite everything you've done, that truth hasn't changed."

For a moment, something flickers in his expression, a crack in his carefully constructed walls of hatred and revenge.

"It's too late for that, *brother*." Ice crystals form around his fingers. "I've spent centuries planning my revenge. I won't let your newfound enlightenment stop me."

The barrier between us crackles with his power, but I don't move away. I see now what Violet would see—not an enemy to be destroyed, but a wounded soul desperate for acceptance.

"I forgive you, Gabriel." The words feel strange on my tongue, but right. "When you're ready to accept that, I'll be here."

His response is a blast of ice magic against the barrier, but I notice his hands trembling.

## Chapter Twenty-Four
# VIOLET

*I really should get used to waking up to the sight of frost patterns dancing across the ceiling.* My fingers trace lazy circles on Jack's bare chest as we lay tangled in silky sheets, watching the morning light filter through the crystalline windows.

"You're staring at me again." Jack's deep voice rumbles beneath my palm.

"Just admiring my work." I trace a line of bite marks along his collarbone, evidence of last night's activities. "You wear my marks well, my Lord Winter."

His hand captures mine, bringing it to his lips. "As you wear mine, my love."

The silvery mark on my arm pulses with warmth at his touch. It's been three days since our wedding, and each morning I discover new aspects of our bond. Like how his magic responds to my emotions, creating delicate ice sculptures when I'm happy or sharp icicles when I'm frustrated.

"The council meeting isn't for hours," Jack murmurs against my skin. His lips trail down my neck, and frost blooms wherever he touches. "Perhaps we could—"

I silence him with a kiss, sliding on top of him, feeling the firm contours of his body align with mine. Magic crackles between us, his winter powers merging with my healing energy in a familiar dance. The temperature drops as desire builds, ice crystals forming in the air around us, a response to the intensity of our connection.

"Fuck the council meeting," I murmur against his lips, my hands exploring the planes of his chest, relishing how his careful control slips and frost spreads across the sheets.

"Such language from my Lady." His voice is a low rumble, but his eyes darken with lust, hands gripping my hips with an urgency that sends a thrill through me.

I can feel the hard length of him pressing against me, insistent and demanding. My own body responds in kind, aching for him, for the union that our powers are desperately seeking.

"Violet," he groans, my name a prayer and a curse on his lips as he bucks beneath me.

I reach between us, wrapping my fingers around him, positioning him at my entrance. His cock slides into me, igniting a rush of sensation that's as overwhelming as it is intoxicating.

The moment he enters me, our powers surge together as we move, the rhythm of our bodies setting a pace that is both frenzied and deliberate. His hands move to my breasts, teasing my nipples into hard peaks, sending jolts of pleasure straight to my core.

Golden healing light mingles with arctic blue, creating aurora-like waves above us, a celestial show for no one but us. I feel his pleasure echo through our bond, a feedback loop that amplifies my own, every thrust, every gasp, resonating deeper than anything I've ever known.

I can feel the rigid control he's famous for unraveling, thread by thread, as I grind against him, our bodies moving in perfect sync. His fingers dig into my hips, pulling me closer, deeper, as if he can't get enough.

The friction between us builds, and with each stroke, I'm certain we're not just fucking—we're merging, two souls becoming one in a dance as old as time.

The room fills with swirling snow and starlight as we chase our release together, the world outside forgotten. His touch is electric, each caress sending jolts of pleasure coursing through me, stoking the fire within me.

I ride him harder, faster, chasing the crest of the wave that's building within me, feeling him swell inside me, hitting that sweet spot that has me seeing stars.

"Come for me, my Lady," he growls, and the command in his voice is my undoing. My orgasm crashes over me, a maelstrom of pleasure that rips a scream from my throat. He follows me over the edge, his cock pulsing inside me as he finds his release, our powers flaring brightly, the room alight with the force of our climax.

We collapse onto the bed, a tangle of limbs, our breaths ragged and our hearts pounding in unison. The magic slowly recedes, leaving us in a warm cocoon, the afterglow making the world outside seem distant and unimportant.

Curled against his chest, I watch the frost patterns he's creating on my skin.

"I never thought I could have this," I admit. "This happiness, this sense of belonging."

"Nor did I." His fingers trace my spine. "I spent centuries believing love would destroy everything I built. Instead..." Ice flowers bloom around us, their petals catching the light. "Instead, you made it stronger."

"We made it stronger," I correct him, pressing a kiss to his jaw. "Together."

His arms tighten around me, and I feel his smile against my hair. The winter kingdom flourishes under our combined magic—my healing abilities complementing his winter powers in ways neither of us expected. Even those who may have initially doubted me have come to accept that their king's mate brings balance rather than destruction.

"What are you thinking about?" Jack's question pulls me from my thoughts.

"How wrong you were about that prophecy." I prop myself up to look at him properly. "Remember how convinced you were that I would ruin everything?"

"I prefer to remember how thoroughly you proved me wrong." His hands slide lower, clearly intent on starting another round of pleasurable activities.

*I could definitely get used to mornings like this.*

I lead Alana down the frosted corridor, watching her eyes widen at each new marvel. Her head swivels back and forth like she's at a tennis match, trying to take in everything at once.

"So, this is where you'll live now?" She reaches out to touch one of the ice sculptures, then yanks her hand back. "Holy shit, it's not even cold!"

"Magic." I wiggle my fingers at her. "The ice here only feels cold if Jack wants it to."

A group of winter fae glide past us, their crystalline wings catching the light. They bow their heads slightly in acknowledgment.

"My Lady," they murmur in unison.

Alana's jaw drops. "Okay, that's going to take some getting used to. You're like... actually damn royalty now?"

"Trust me, I'm still adjusting too." I guide her toward the kitchens. "Wait until you see where they make the food."

The kitchen doors swing open to reveal organized chaos. Frost sprites dart between stations, carrying trays of sparkling delicacies. The head cook, Marigold, looks up from where she's directing the controlled mayhem.

"My Lady!" Her smile brightens the already gleaming room. "And this must be the famous Alana we've heard so much about."

"Famous?" Alana elbows me. "What exactly have you been saying about me?"

"Only the good stuff." I snag a pastry from a passing tray. "Like how you're the best nurse in Colorado and saved my ass more times than I can count."

Marigold claps her hands. "You must try our winter berry tarts. They're made with berries that only grow in eternal frost."

She presents Alana with a crystal plate. The tarts shimmer like they're dusted with diamonds.

"These are incredible." Alana's eyes roll back in pleasure as she takes a bite. "After all these fancy meals, Vi, you'll never touch hospital food again. These gourmet dishes will have ruined you for life."

"That's fair."

A commotion at the door draws our attention. Several kitchen staff scramble to bow as Jack enters, his presence immediately commanding the room.

"Ah, there you are." He approaches us, nodding politely to Alana. "I trust you're enjoying the tour?"

"Your Majesty." Alana attempts an awkward curtsy that makes me snort.

"Please, just Jack is fine. You're practically family now."

"Family that you tried to freeze to death during that storm," I remind him, but there's no heat in my words.

"A regrettable misunderstanding." His lips quirk up at the corners. "And not within my control. Though it did work out rather well in the end."

Alana looks between us, shaking her head. "You two are disgustingly cute together. Who knew the Lord of Winter was such a softie?"

"I'm the one who had to watch you and Brad make eyes at each other for months. Talk about wanting to vomit," I tease.

The temperature drops slightly, and I pat Jack's arm. "She's teasing us, love. No need to frost the pastries."

The warmth returns as Jack relaxes, though he maintains his regal posture. "Perhaps we should continue the tour? The library is particularly impressive this time of day."

"Yes, let's go see the library." I tug Alana's arm, eager to show her my favorite room in the castle. "You won't believe the collection they have."

*God, I sound like such a nerd right now.*

Alana grabs another tart before following us. "Is everything in here made of ice?"

"Not everything." I trail my fingers along the smooth white walls as we walk. "Though Jack does have a flair for the dramatic when it comes to interior design."

Jack's shoulder brushes mine. "I prefer to think of it as maintaining aesthetic consistency."

"See what I have to deal with?" I roll my eyes at Alana. "He talks like he swallowed a thesaurus."

The massive library doors swing open at Jack's gesture, revealing towering shelves that stretch up into shadows. Sunlight streams through stained glass windows, casting rainbow patterns across ancient tomes and scrolls.

Alana's mouth falls open. "Holy shit. This makes the Library of Congress look like a magazine rack."

"Many of these texts are the only surviving copies in any realm." Jack's voice carries that note of pride I've come to recognize.

I catch him watching me as I show my favorite reading nook to Alana—a window seat lined with furs and cushions. His expression softens when our eyes meet, and warmth blooms in my chest despite the perpetual winter chill.

"Violet practically lives in here." Jack's formal posture relaxes slightly. "I often find her asleep surrounded by medical texts and histories."

"That tracks." Alana examines a shelf of glowing manuscripts. "She used to fall asleep in the hospital library during breaks."

"I did not!"

"You drooled on three different medical journals."

My cheeks heat. "Those books were boring. These are actually interesting."

*These books feel different under my fingers, almost alive with their own energy.*

I trace the spine of an ancient healing tome, watching the silver script shimmer at my touch. "At least these books respond when I read them. Sometimes they even glow."

Alana leans closer to examine the text. "Wait, are those words actually moving?"

"Living knowledge." Jack's voice carries that teacher-tone he gets when sharing his realm's mysteries. "The texts adapt to show what the reader needs to learn."

"That would have made nursing school so much easier." Alana reaches for the book, then hesitates. "Can I...?"

I nod. "It's safe. They only bite if you try to steal them."

"She's joking." Jack's cool fingers brush my shoulder. "Mostly."

Alana carefully opens the book, gasping as the pages illuminate with diagrams of human anatomy overlaid with flowing lines of magical energy.

"This is incredible! Is this how you see patients now?"

"Something like that." I peer over her shoulder at the familiar patterns. "It's helped me understand how mortal and magical healing can work together. See those golden threads? That's life force - what we'd call vital signs in medical terms."

"Your understanding of both worlds has already improved our healing practices considerably." Jack's praise warms me more than I'd like to admit.

"I just wish I'd known about this sooner. Think of all the patients we could have helped."

Alana's expression grows serious. "Speaking of p atients..." She closes the book gently. "The hospital's been asking when you're coming back."

My stomach twists. *I knew this conversation was coming.* "I can't exactly commute between realms for my shifts."

"You could, though, right?" Alana's eyes dart to Jack.

"It's not that simple." *How do I explain that I'm needed here? That I'm finally where I belong?*

"What she means," Jack steps closer, his presence steady and reassuring, "is that her duties here require significant attention. The integration of mortal and magical healing is delicate work."

I squeeze his hand, grateful for the support. "I'm not abandoning nursing, Alana. I'm just... practicing on a different scale now."

"But you'll visit, right?" Alana's eyes shine with unshed tears.

I wrap my arms around her. "Of course. Jack's already working on a way for me to travel more easily between realms."

"Good, because I need my best friend." She pulls back, wiping her eyes. "Especially now that I've sworn off men forever."

"What? Since when?"

"Since Brad." She slumps against the library wall. "Found him with one of the new surgical residents last week."

"I'll take that as my cue to leave," Jack grins and makes an exaggerated bow. I give him a quick nod before turning my attention back to Alana.

My hands curl into fists. "*What*? That absolute—"

"It's fine." She waves off my anger. "I'm done. No more relationships. No more dating. Just me, my career, and occasional wine nights with you."

"Alana..."

"Don't give me that look. I mean it this time." She straightens her spine. "Some of us aren't destined for magical fairy tale romances with winter kings."

*If she only knew what I went through to get here.*

"Besides," she continues, "after seeing all this—" she gestures at our surroundings "—how could any normal guy compare? What's the point?"

A chill draft whistles through the library, making the pages of nearby books flutter.

"Speaking of magical beings..." I bite my lip. "There's something else you should know. About Gabriel."

Her expression darkens. "The guy who tried to kill you and Jack?"

"He's... contained. In the dungeons below."

"You have *dungeons*?" She shakes her head. "Of course, you have dungeons. Wait—isn't that dangerous, keeping him here?"

"Jack has him under powerful binding spells. But. .." I hesitate, remembering Gabriel's wild eyes and bitter words. "He's Jack's brother. Half-brother. It's complicated."

"Sounds like a mess." She wraps her arms around herself. "Promise me you'll be careful? I don't trust anyone who'd try to hurt their own family like that."

"I promise." I touch the silvery mark on my arm. "But you should have seen him, Alana. He looked so... broken. Like someone who's been alone too long."

"Don't." She points a finger at me. "I know that tone. That's your 'someone needs healing' voice. Some people can't be fixed, Vi."

*Maybe. But everyone deserves a chance at redemption.*

## Chapter Twenty-Five

# JACK

The month after our wedding, I stand at the grand windows of my chambers—*our* chambers now. Violet's warmth still lingers on my skin, her scent of vanilla and frost flowers permeating the air. Something has shifted in my realm. It has been a slow but steady shift.

Sunlight streams through the ice crystal windows, casting rainbow prisms across the floor. The eternal darkness that plagued my kingdom for years has lifted. *How did I never notice how oppressive that darkness was?*

"The ice walls are melting." Violet's arms wrap around my waist from behind, her chin resting against my shoulder.

I cover her hands with mine. "No, not melting like before. Transforming."

Where once stood impenetrable barriers of solid ice, delicate frost patterns now dance across transparent crystal walls. The fortress I built to keep others out has become a palace that welcomes the light.

"Your people seem different, too." She moves to stand beside me, watching the winter fae below in the courtyard.

She's right. My subjects no longer hurry through their tasks with heads bowed. They pause to chat, to laugh.

A group of younger fae are even creating ice sculptures together, their magic combining in ways I've never witnessed before.

"It's you." I turn to face her, tracing the silvery mate mark on her arm. "Remember, soul healing magic doesn't just work on individuals? It works on realms too."

Violet's power pulses beneath my touch, warm and inviting. "We did this together. Your winter magic needed my warmth, just like I needed your strength."

A messenger appears at our door, frost swirling around their feet.

"My Lord, My Lady. The human delegates have arrived through the new passage."

*The passage.* Another change that appeared with our union—stable pathways between realms that don't require exhausting magical transport.

"Ready to be our bridge, little mate?"

Violet's eyes sparkle with determination. "Born ready. Though if you keep calling me 'little mate' in front of the human delegates, I'll have to remind you just how *not little* I can be."

Magic surges between us at her words, causing frost patterns to spiral across the floor. Even my power responds differently to her now. It's playful where it once was rigid, warm where it once was bitterly cold.

The eternal winter hasn't ended—this is still the Winter Kingdom after all. But now it's a winter of crisp morning frost and gentle snowfall, of midnight auroras and crystalline beauty. A winter that invites rather than repels.

Just like its king.

---

Looking for more *Yule Be Mine* Holiday Monster Romance?

***Kraved by Krampus*** by Jewel Hayes and Alexa Ashe
***Kissed by the Kitsune*** by Lexi Lennox
***Bitten by the Winter Vampire*** by H.C. Hunter
***Tempted by the Yule Lads*** by Annie Black
***Caught by the Christmas Cat*** by Lexi Lennox

Click the image above, or also available at author.alexaashe.com/yulebemineseries

# WHAT'S NEXT

Thank you for reading *Jilted by Jack Frost!*

Did this book give you all the feels?

Reviews are the high-fives of the literary world, and you'd be my hero by leaving one. Only a small percentage of readers take the time to leave reviews—you could be among that exceptional group who helps others discover the magic within these pages.

Plus, they make my day. So, please share your thoughts!

Or even just taking a few seconds to drop a star rating is hugely appreciated! You should see one right about this point in the book....

- Alexa

Did you enjoy this book? Want to see more? Then you'll LOVE the rest of the books in the **Yule Be Mine Series**, a completed series of 6 stand-alone holiday, wintery monster romance books.

Here's a sneak peek of my next book in the series, *Kraved by Krampus*

I glare at the empty page before me, my mind as blank as the page itself. Not a single idea worth putting down comes to my head.

My latest manuscript—"Mistletoe Miracles and Manhattan"—is due in three weeks, and I've got nothing.

Nothing except the same tired tropes my readers expect: plucky small-town girl, big city Christmas party, conveniently handsome CEO.

"God, I can't write this drivel anymore." I slam the notebook shut and rub my ink-stained fingers over my face, forgetting about my reading glasses until they smudge. Perfect.

The cabin's kitchen beckons. Midnight stress-baking has become my new normal, though my agent would have a fit if she knew I wasn't writing. My "Queen of Christmas Cheer" brand doesn't allow for 2 AM cookie binges.

I pull out mixing bowls, flour flying as I attack the ingredients. "Sweet, wholesome, uplifting," I mutter, cracking eggs with more force than necessary. "That's what they want. That's what sells. That's what pays the bills."

My mother's old recipe book falls open to devil's food cake. I almost laugh at the irony—even my subconscious is rebelling against all this sugary sweetness.

The beautiful kitchen seems to expand around me as I work, counter space appearing just where I need it. I'm too frustrated to question the convenient layout. My brain flickers momentarily to the incredible bargain I lucked into for this stunning last-minute rental, but my thoughts snap right back to my troubles.

My latest hero and heroine dance through my mind—both so perfectly bland I can barely tell them apart.

"Would it kill my readers if someone got pushed into the snow instead of falling gracefully?" I ask the mixing bowl. "Or if the Christmas party ended in delicious scandal instead of a chaste kiss under the mistletoe?"

"What is wrong with me?" I mutter, cracking eggs with more force than necessary. The shells splinter in my hands. "Just write the damn book. Girl meets boy, they fall in love, Christmas magic happens. How hard can it be?"

But it feels hollow. Empty. Like I'm just going through the motions.

The mixing bowl scrapes against the counter with a harsh ceramic sound as I cream butter and sugar together, watching the ingredients transform into a pale, fluffy mass. My hands work on autopilot as I start to add the flour, sending little puffs of white dust into the air with each measured cup I pour in.

My editor's voice echoes in my head. "Your readers expect heartwarming holiday romance, Noelle. That's your brand."

I fold in chocolate chips with sharp, angry movements. The dough feels too stiff under my hands, but I keep working it. Just like I keep forcing myself to write stories that feel increasingly false.

"Come on, Noelle," I whisper to myself. "You're supposed to be the Queen of Christmas Cheer." But even as I say it, doubt creeps in. Am I really cut out for this? My public image as a sweet romance author feels like a straitjacket sometimes, constraining me from exploring darker, more passionate stories.

The oven preheats faster than I expected. I've got chocolate under my fingernails and flour in my hair, but at least baking makes sense. Unlike my career, where I'm trapped in a prison of my own making—each bestseller adding another bar to my cage of wholesome expectations.

"Mother would know what to say," I whisper to the empty kitchen. My fingers trace the ink stains on my hands—evidence of all the failed attempts at writing today. The first batch of cookies goes in, and the kitchen fills with the scent of vanilla and chocolate.

But even stress-baking isn't helping tonight. The words still won't come, and the darkness I want to explore in my writing keeps pushing against the boundaries of what's expected from me.

I lean against the counter, watching the cookies bake through the oven window, and wonder how much longer I can keep pretending to be someone I'm not.

A gust of wind rattles the kitchen windows, and I swear the temperature drops. My tea, sitting forgotten on the counter, still steaming despite being hours old.

My phone vibrates against the counter, Victoria's name lighting up the screen. Great. Just what I need right now, another pressure check-in from my publisher.

"Noelle, darling." Victoria's voice drips honey, but I catch the frost underneath. "Tell me you have good news about our Christmas miracle."

I stare at my chocolate-smeared hands. "I'm... working on it."

"Working on it?" The temperature seems to drop through the phone. "Darling, we need more than 'working on it.' The holiday season waits for no one. We need to get them ready to go now."

"I know, I just—"

"Your readers are counting on you. You're their beacon of Christmas joy, their guarantee of happily ever after." Victoria's voice shifts, somehow both stern and sympathetic. "Remember what happened with Holly Winter's latest book? She tried to 'experiment' with darker themes. Her sales tanked."

My stomach knots. "That's not—"

"The market knows what it wants, especially during the holidays. Light. Sweet. Wholesome." Each word falls like an icicle. "You do want to keep your contract, don't you?"

I grip the phone tighter. The manuscript hidden in my bag seems to pulse with dark energy, calling to me. "Of course."

"Wonderful. Then I expect fifty pages of pure Christmas magic by Monday. No surprises, no darkness, just the Noelle Goodheart special that made you famous." Victoria pauses. "And darling? Maybe lay off the midnight baking. You sound tired."

The line goes dead. I set the phone down with shaking hands, wondering how she knew about the baking. The kitchen feels colder now, and my tea has finally stopped steaming.

The cookies in the oven have burned.

---

I flop down on the couch in the living room and open up my laptop. The flashing line taunts me. Write something sweet, something wholesome. A meet-cute at a Christmas tree farm. A snowball fight that ends in kisses.

My fountain pen rolls across the coffee table—though I swear I didn't touch it. When I grab it, the ink catches the lamplight, sparkling like fresh snow. Must be the new brand I'm trying. I grab my notebook, and my ink-stained fingers are a familiar comfort as I begin to jot down ideas. But the words refuse to flow. Every sentence feels forced, every scene overly sweet.

"Focus," I mutter, but my eyes drift to the bag where my other manuscript hides. The real story. Dark and wild, full of ancient winter magic and a feared deity who—

No. I force my attention back to the blank page. Write something. Anything.

*Jenny's heart soared as she hung the last ornament on the tree. This Christmas would be perfect, especially with—*

Papers flutter across the table, scattering my notes even though the window is sealed tight. The lamp flickers, and shadows dance across the walls like restless spirits seeking escape.

My secret manuscript seems to pulse from across the room, calling to me with an intensity that makes my fingers itch and my heart race. Each beat matches the steady thrum of dark possibilities hidden within those pages.

I cross the room and yank my bag open, pulling out the handwritten pages. The ink shimmers darker than I remember, the words more alive. Stories of Krampus, the winter demon who punishes the wicked. Not the sanitized version—the real legends. The ones that make your blood run cold and your heart race.

Victoria's words echo in my head like a mantra I can't escape. *Light. Sweet. Wholesome.* Everything I'm supposed to be, everything my readers expect from the Queen of Christmas Cheer.

This manuscript will ruin me. My career, my reputation, everything I've carefully built over the years. All those book signings, interviews, Instagram posts portraying the perfect holiday author, gone in an instant if anyone sees these words.

The fireplace crackles, flames dancing with an almost hypnotic rhythm. It would be so easy to feed the pages to the fire, watch my darkness turn to ash. Return to safe, sweet stories that sell, the kind Victoria loves to publish. The kind that keep me comfortable and secure.

My hands shake as I approach the fireplace, the manuscript clutched to my chest like a guilty secret. The pages feel hot against my skin, burning with words I never meant to write. One motion, that's all it would take. Just open my fingers and let gravity do the rest.

I extend my arms, holding the pages over the flames. The fire leaps higher, as if reaching for them, hungry for the forbidden stories I've poured onto these pages. My heart pounds so hard I can feel it in my throat.

The heat caresses my palms, a lover's touch urging me to give in, to let these dangerous words dissolve into nothing but smoke and ash. Every muscle in my body trembles with indecision.

A cold wind howls outside the cabin, and the lights go out.

**Read more in *Kraved by Krampus*—my other book in the *Yule Be Mine* steamy monster romance series today!**

---

**If you liked my book, you can also grab my free book *Cursed in Love*!** It's about a witch in hiding and the handsome prince she tried to curse!

ALEXA ASHE
CURSED
IN
LOVE
AN ENEMIES TO LOVERS ROYAL ROMANCE

# ABOUT AUTHOR

I've always been fascinated by the magical worlds that exist only in the imagination. In fact, I once tried to cast a spell on my math teacher to make him forget about homework - it didn't work, but it did inspire me to start writing my own stories.

When I'm not busy creating new characters and stories, I'm usually snuggled up with a good book and a hot cup of tea (or a glass of wine, depending on the time of day). Just don't disturb me while I'm in the middle of a particularly juicy chapter - I probably won't even hear you anyway.

I'm inspired by so many things - nature, history, mythology, and the human experience, just to name a few. I pour my heart into every story I write, and I'm always humbled by the positive feedback I receive from readers.

If you've ever read one of my books, thank you from the bottom of my heart - it means more to me than you'll ever know!

Alexa Ashe

https://www.facebook.com/authoralexaashe